WHEN CHR

by James Eric Davison, Ph.D.
Copyright, James Eric Davison, 11/2010

Dedicated to my father, Dexter Davison, who taught me that people are capable of infinite good and infinite evil.

We begin by acknowledging that we all had a hand in this.

-1-

The day finally came: Father Sperry opened the 170-year-old parish hall door for the last time. The air was dank inside; the AC had long since ceased to work. There was no money- the last worshipper left the week before. Sperry eyed the old altar at the end of the hall. Spirits danced in the eves- music of eras come and gone played- but no one heard.

Father Sperry had spent his career in the ministry making straight the crooked ways of men and institutions. He was no stranger to adversity; he'd suffered great pain in his family of origin, his father succumbing to disease. He'd sown his own wild oats in his youth, and he knew the bite of excess. Sperry, a learned man, a man with a head for facts and discipline, just KNEW if he was ernest enough, if he didn't miss a detail, that he could bring this congregation, like all the others, back to life. What baffled him was that people always did what they wanted to do, and this ran counter to his logic. Therefore, defeat must be his and his alone.

Sperry was heavy with grief. The week before he'd gone to the diocesan gathering where the new bishop celebrated the new "Pantheon of Virtues", extolling the myths of Budah, Krishna, Mohammad, and Christ. "Jesus Christ", said Sperry, "is dead?"

-2-

Erik opened the door to the house heavy with anticipation-- he'd just returned from the war in Afghanistan. He had a decided limp--just missed getting his leg blown off from an IED explosion. He still had most of his foot, but lost part of his right calf. Perpetual pain. Now 60, the Guard was done with him, and he with it. Troops were streaming home now as the president said the war was "unwinnable". Erik thought hard about those kids he saw dead in Kabul--and he feared for the Afghan families who backed the U.S.-financed regime. They'd begged to come to the U.S. They'd begged for their children's lives-- only to be kicked away from the giant transports revving their engines for take-off.

Erik knew the Guard needed somebody to help the soldiers coming home. They'd lost so much---

Erik's dogs rushed him at the door with unbridled gratitude for his return. What JOY to see their faces! They about knocked him over! Erik hardly noticed the grass standing tall in the yard from neglect. He shuffled past the stacks of mail left unopened on the hallway floor. He headed for the family gathering place, the T.V. room, anxious to be embraced and loved.

"Oh hi, dear, we're watching Glee. They finally showed a gay sex scene--everyone knew it was going to happen---"

"Uh, Autumn, you've grown so!"

"Hey, Dad", she said still eying Glee on the wall. Pizza boxes littered the room and the computers were downloading something lengthy. "Can you take me and my friends to the mall after this?"

Erik's heart sank as he looked into the two faces of the women closest to him in the whole world. And their eyes never left the T.V. to meet his.

Arpert, a disheveled, aching caricature of a harassed man, walked into his classroom at St. Peter's School for the last time. He'd been told to clear out his desk of all personal effects and be off the property before the boys came up from breakfast. Thirty-nine years a master. Thirty-nine years of teaching, coaching, mentoring brought shamefully to this hollow climax. He wasn't even allowed to say goodbye to the kids. St. Peter's had recently abandoned weekly chapel exercises as the introduction of Islam and Zen into what was once a Christian observance had drawn litigation. Not that anyone missed chapel--teachers and students alike were happy to see it go--better to quietly observe diversity than to extol one god. After all, a truly pluralistic society must allow all observances---

Arpert remembered his father's dismissal from a similar private school job in 1972. It was so hard to bear after all he had given. Arpert stuck it out in this great school all those years; thrust and parry--keeping up the good fight--for the kids--for his family--for the glory of teaching the way he knew best. Socrates would have been proud! In his day Arpert had been the jaunty, avant-garde teacher to beat them all; so adventurous, so bold in the classroom, so deep in his probing of the issues of the day as they related to history. He couldn't be stopped.

Today Arpert stood trembling with self-doubt. Arpert's bout with alcoholism was not unusual for tired, old masters--great educational institutions used to work with them--they were cherished, revered icons, many of them. And they were nurtured back to health--always cared for and always honored.

Arpert was considered an expensive liability. And he dared question the chapel policy. Now his "illness", his surgeries, his lateness, his combative teaching style, his obvious love for the students and their love for him--were messy, expensive liabilities for the streamlined, predictable new administration of power-consensus.

Arpert dragged himself up the hall and stared at the gigantic face of the sitting U.S. president filling the entire space at the end of the hallway. He wondered--what now? With a packed supreme court, a 51st state, and a proposal surfacing in Congress to end two-term limits for the Presidency--and this visage threatening to replace religious icons….what's next?

Arpert closed his eyes and heard MOTHER admonish him for letting his facial hair get so scruffy, Mom died just the past year---a sudden stroke in the middle of the night. "Good thing", he silenced her--"Good thing you're not here to see this, Mom!" Mother and Dad were the toast of the faculty at St.

Peter's in 1945: the shiny young couple from New York City with such promise and enthusiasm! They'd done the USO circuit with a drama Dad had written. Victory and hope were in everyone's hearts! What a contrast. Arpert's taste of irony was like ground glass.

Gene was in the airport in Taipai, Taiwan when he read the news on the front page of the New York Times: "Christian Protesters Tear-gassed at 16th and Pennsylvania Avenue Yesterday! Violence feared by Homeland Security. President speaks out in favor of multicultural pantheon to be dedicated on the Mall in D.C."

Gene was a well-published educator of many years---mostly in independent schools. He was sleek, polished, with the right words, the most acceptable turn of a phrase, and the best fabrics on his moderately-toned frame. He married an image consultant who turned pillow talk into power tutorials. Gene was the model of corporate finesse. He was irresistible.

Gene's retirement from the headmastership of a well-financed southern school propelled him into a lucrative consultancy. Traveling the globe, Gene brought together the best and the brightest--at some cost---to extol the virtues of private education for the new elite in emerging economies. "We can't let Christ-worship be our center of gravity anymore", he asserted to himself--"we have a great BIG world out there, and if we are all going to get along we have to praise the qualities of all gods and beliefs". It just made financial sense.

Dave had just gotten off the phone with the local news team from Channel 13, and his face was ashen. The offending teacher was still sitting in front of him. He expected the police any minute. "Tell me again---step by step--what happened in class?" The stunned teacher couldn't even muster tears anymore. Powerless over her life, powerless over her fate, powerless over her working conditions--she just rambled out the stages of the latest classroom catastrophe at Dave's school: the homeroom bell rang--the kids poured in the classroom--they started mouthing off--she grabbed her camera phone and started to record "to save her own ass". The kids grabbed one girl--they beat her down to the floor--they ripped her clothes off--the teacher made terrified chirps and gasps but said nothing--the girl screamed for help as boys held her down---two other girls grabbed a ruler and jabbed it repeatedly into the screaming girl's vagina. The boys holding her legs cheered and shouted--the camera rocked and blurred as the teacher ran…

Dave asked the frightened woman where she went, and she couldn't even remember. Another teacher found her trembling in the corner of the teachers' lounge. All the kids from homeroom dispersed, the victim lay bleeding and screaming until a teacher across the hall finally summoned the nurse. "Don't EVER touch a student--summon the nurse or assistant principal!"--words from Public School Teaching 101: I.E. never intervene to save anyone. This twisted spawn of legal drubbings had morphed into teachers saving themselves and doing personal video recordings of classroom violence until they could get away.

No one had dared pray in that school since the late 20th century.

Dave stared ahead into the wall. "How many days until retirement? Will I get demoted? Will I be sued?" The police arrived, seized the cellphone from the teacher, and they took HER away. Dave feared the next morning's papers like he'd never feared a day in his life.

Josi had given her life to Christ in college in 1973. A full year of sex, drugs and drama had left her bloated and barely passing school. Intervarsity, the campus Christian fellowship, came along and drew her in. It was HAPPY-CLAPPY JESUS, WAVE YOUR ARMS, AND WORRY THE POOR SINNERS ever since!

She'd married a reborn construction worker, a reformed LSD-head, to the dismay of her well-educated parents. She had by him four children. All were carted off to every church event humanly possible, they played in the worship bands, did all the youth events, and felt the rod of discipline so very popular with the REBORN SET. "Gettin' Old Testament" with your kids was a huge relief for Jesus-Freak parents who needed control in this world of licentiousness. The kids lived like over-exposed Amish--split between two worlds and totally confused about their own emotions. Normal feelings could get you into trouble.

One day Josi's oldest boy got enraged with his youth pastor and took a swing at him. The youth pastor got the boy outside. No one heard from the lad after that, and the pastor said the boy ran off. Eighteen hours later the boy was found hanging by the neck from a tree off in the woods.

It was deemed a suicide….the boy was trouble. Josi never felt the same again about her religion. At sea once again in her faith life--her other kids began to drift away.

Josi found a job. Now she felt "complete" at last. Her church did not object.

A Hamas defector gets interviewed on National Public Radio. The host asks some pithy questions about the man's intent in leaving Hamas, and he quotes the Koran in Ch.9 "where it speaks about the right of every Muslim to kill the infidel". The host on NPR asks if he believes that is true Islamic belief, and the defector states, "Yes!" The host gets very perturbed on the air stating that "she has interviewed many Islamic scholars who stated definitively that it is a misinterpretation of the Koran" and she dismisses her guest as "misinformed".

It has come to this: all religions carry equal value in the politically-correct order. It actually means to them that the MYTH of each religion has equal merit---as a scholarly archaeological pursuit---God is an abstract construct---Christ a forgotten stepchild.

"Jesus Christ!", exclaims the sexual partner of Henry VIII's unfaithful wife on Showtime. This T.V. repeat, a favorite of the wine-sipping intelligensia, has played for years. Swearing? Exclamation during orgasm? Taunt of the damned? No, just effective punctuation; a laughable irony. Anything but the Son of God. "Oh lighten up! The Church has!"

Feeling like he is curled up in the dry-boned grip of the angel of death, Father Sperry sank into his leather office swivel-chair and stared at the blank computer screen on his desk. "Is it true? Have I struggled for nothing? Is Christ just a footnote in the millennia of mankind's search for meaning? And now, OFFICIALLY, just one of the state pantheon? I've struggled, cried, denied myself, marched, raised my boys, remained faithful, true, scholarly, in pain--laughed at--diminished by my "peers" in the CHURCH--all for this?" Burying his face in his hands he was too fragile to cry. A lone heave--a dry sob--a shudder to the bones. And empty.

Drooping, the black-clad pastor dared not even look up at the mirror on the wall behind the chair where countless counselees had sat LOOKING FOR HOPE. He studied his face in his mind's eye--where---where in that empty head was HOPE?

Father Sperry had long since quit blaming himself as failing to save his flock. All the games, gimmicks, pleadings, guiltings, reminding, visits, calls, sermons--wave on wave---spasms of energy at the last--with only dying embers faintly glowing in all that darkened ash. Yes, Sperry felt encased in damp, trash-filled ash--looking for signs of life in all this. "Ashes to ashes, dust to dust". The spark of light fading in the aging preacher's eyes.

There really wasn't much to say as the cops stuffed Father Sperry's boy into the squad car. He was caught red-handed. Sperry didn't even have words of hope, nor anger, nor disappointment. Nature had simply taken its course: without Christ there was no definition--no purpose--no reason to behave. Was his faith so fragile? Didn't that guy still merit consideration by his boy? Was violence just another societal pitfall? Could blind rage now be justified?

Sperry knew a police psychologist would evaluate his boy. And likely it would come clear: once the parents gave up, the boy saw no reason to do the right thing. And so, since the lad had gone to and left college and was now living under their care--they would no doubt be blamed for this.

"What have we become?" agonized Sperry. "Just rats in a cage pressing a lever for more and more stimulation?" Yet there wasn't any fun.

"My poor, dear wife!" For a few moments, lost in self-pity, Sperry neglected the one person alive who NEVER failed--who ALWAYS did right by him and everyone else. His beloved wife, Olive.

Sperry gathered himself, ran to the rectory, threw open the front doors and frantically shouted her name: "Olive! Olive, where are you, dear Olive?!" Silence greeted him outside the pounding in his ears. Sperry darted in and out of doorways looking in all her usual spots--NO OLIVE!

Father Sperry was typically a thinking kind of man--not even passionate outbursts and wild conjecture--but now in this day----this hour--this moment of utter despair--all he could muster was a vision of Olive alone and suffering terribly. He knew not why.

A moan from deep inside him left Sperry's gut, and he sank to his knees raising his fists heavenward. "No, not Olive!"

A whimper, a calling whimper popped out of the bathroom upstairs in the mansion. Sperry found his legs and raced up the stairs with his eyes fixed on the unlit open bathroom. "Olive!"

Olive was splayed sideways wrenched between the toilet and the bathtub. Her leg had slipped out from under her as she rushed to get out of the tub. Fortunately the head wound was not serious, but her leg was clearly broken. She smiled into his eyes.

Erik's vision for a homecoming was shattered. He had not the energy to object, and the home front was a ship long a-sail without him. That night-- as in the year before he deployed-- he slept alone. His wife said his snoring was intolerable. Erik hadn't even been able to excite his wife's passions before he left for combat. Why should she bother now? She always made it clear she preferred to be left alone when it came to sex--so WHAT THE HELL?!

A thousand dollars in cash called out louder than any desire to look for affection at home. Sure--THEY'd take the cash---drag him to the mall---and make him wait for hours while they spent every nickel. Later his wife would explain away her disaffection as "needing to adjust to him being home"-- she'd used this before when he'd been gone merely a week. All Erik could muster was visions of homecomings that melted painfully before this stark reality: he was merely a fixture in the home.

Erik quietly withdrew out the door, put the dogs in the passenger seat and drove toward the truck stops along the highway. Surely SOMEONE would touch him for his money there. As the car pulled off the girls giggled at the all-male sex scene on Glee. "It's about the music after all…"

She was helped gasping into the coffee shop. She, a journalist from London, pregnant and in agony from snapping her ankle in a pothole crossing the street, was gently rested in an armchair and given ice in a towel. A coffee girl wrapped the towel over her injured and bloated foot and bound it with an ace wrap she'd dug out of her purse. The poor English woman declared that she was alone in Baltimore covering an immunology conference. Everyone looked at the ankle and advised she get to the ER. John Hopkins was just blocks away, and the coffee girl talked with the English woman about options. Folks advised against an ambulance as the lady had no insurance. Calling the cab company revealed that no passenger could be picked up in town from a phone call. A coffee boy hailed a cab and asked if they could take the poor woman to the hospital. No, for liability purposes. Staff at the coffee shop reasoned that her hotel, two blocks away, could give her a ride on their shuttle. When called, the hotel declined as their liability would not allow them to offer help.

The coffee girl apologized to the English woman for the sad state of her country. She expressed shame at her litigious, amoral society. She asked the writer to write about this once she recovered. Finally the coffee boy brought his own car out front; he would be the Good Samaritan.

The afternoon soaps were interrupted by frenzied network banter fresh from newsrooms in New York City: No one could believe the reports that had come in---- but apparently some kind of large explosion had taken place on the MALL in D.C. just south of the White House. The blast was sufficient to topple the Washington Monument, blow in the front of the Smithsonian, but the White House, Lincoln Memorial, and Capitol stood. The trouble was, people were dropping fast--well beyond the blast zone. Cars, busses, bicyclists, pedestrians all stopped dead with some motors still running. A chopper had spun out over the Mall and crashed. News helicopters refused to fly. Police were trying to get people out---many D.C. police simply got in their cars and took off for the suburbs. News cameras broadcasting live were dropping as scenes of reporters gasping for air spun out of focus.

A dirty bomb had unleashed some as-yet-unknown pestilence over Washington---and the winds were carrying the fog over the Capitol, Supreme Court into the East. Last heard, the president had been in the Oval Office working. No word on him yet. No word from the cabinet either.

Helicopters were seen scrambling out of the Pentagon flying south and west--no official word from the Joint Chiefs---

Silence from the Hill--the White House---the Pentagon---no official statements yet from anyone in Washington. Who was in charge?

Panic-stricken, the news anchors speculated as to who would be in charge given any number of possible scenarios. Strangely there was no grief-- no empathy--no uttered concern for any of our government officials or their families in Washington---almost as if all those sympathies had been used up--worn out--cheapened and rendered invalid emotions long ago.

The cable news outlets oddly enough began interviewing each other--almost in alliance---to fend off fears of dissolution of authority. Finally Fox News in Baltimore brought the governor of Maryland on the air. He was dressed in tennis clothes when he uttered these words:

"Ladies and gentlemen, fellow Marylanders, all Americans within the sound of my voice--I have the sad duty to announce to you that an explosion near the Washington Monument on the Mall in D.C. has spread some toxic substance over the city. There appear to be mass casualties. Efforts to reach the White House have failed. Efforts to reach Congress, in session, have failed. The Joint Chiefs have not answered. I am mobilizing the National Guard to assist in the evacuation of areas in Maryland within a 30-mile radius north and west of D.C., and I understand the governor of Virginia is acting similarly to secure areas south of D.C. At present, with prevailing winds coming from the West, counties east of D.C. cannot be approached. We are monitoring winds carefully, and I encourage all Marylanders to make an orderly effort to exit the state for points north and west. I myself was in Baltimore at the time of the explosion. My family [choking] are in Annapolis, and I have not been able to reach them. Presumably the pestilence has engulfed them by now---but we must not abandon hope. Therefore--while we evacuate--we keep our cellphones on---our hearts open and we hope for the best. If you have a god---I would call upon that god now for the safe keeping of our loved ones."

With that the governor stepped aside taking no questions. Folks in the studio in Baltimore started to speculate about the winds shifting northeast, and one anchor said goodbye---he was going to get his family and head for PA.

-13-

Erik rushed home, the radio blurting fear; he never made it to the truck stops---he'd always listened to talk radio, and the usual anti-liberal fare had been preempted suddenly by the news flash: the national capital was incommunicado. Erik knew a terrorist strike had crippled D.C. --he also knew he'd be re-deployed any moment now. Now his instincts drove him home: DUTY to protect his family came like an onrushing tidal wave overpowering any lingering familial resentments. He was trying to raise his wife on her cell phone--she never paid it any attention. He dismissed texting his daughter as the State had outlawed texting while driving, and Erik had fallen out of practice. Besides --- getting home was priority-- QUICK!

Erik burst through the front door of the house and shouted for his wife and daughter--the dogs ran through the house wild with excitement. No answer from the girls--he rounded the kitchen and found them still in their repose watching recorded T.V. They barely looked sideways as Erik shouted for them to listen--finally he hit the T.V. power button and stared at their shocked disbelief -- not at what he was saying -- but that their episode had been interrupted. A look of disdain shadowed his daughter's features--this no longer gave Erik pangs of hurt---she'd told him years before that he didn't really ACT like a father--so why should she defer to him?

Erik was relentless -- he spilled the awful truth: D.C. was attacked and in a blackout---a dangerous atmosphere was traveling east--and could move slightly northward in their direction. THEY HAD TO GET OUT! The roads weren't yet jammed---THEY HAD TO GO NOW!

Mother and daughter raised protest. Daughter had to text her friends first, and mother needed clothes. Erik exploded: "NO! Get the leashes, grab the dogs, and get in the car! There is NO time!" Erik's wife grabbed her purse and coat, and daughter dug in the couch for her phone charger. This might later prover to be a life-saver, nodded Erik. Still he yelled, "No time, let's GO!"

-14-

Fox News Baltimore was on the road broadcasting concern for the people of Maryland. Calls were going out repeatedly trying to raise up the governor again. He needed to speak to the people, to reassure them. Rumors had it he had left the state for points north or west. Fox called it shameful neglect of public duty. Being a democrat didn't help.

Suddenly the newscasters cut to Richmond, VA where Fox news was covering the Virginia capitol. The governor of Virginia had convened the state representatives and government agency heads. Fox had word that the governor was about to take some bold strokes. Let's listen in:

"Fellow Virginians, I stand before you at a critical hour. By now it should be apparent to all that disaster in the form of a devastating "dirty bomb" has befallen our nation's capital. So far we have little information on the exact nature of the weapon, but preliminary reports suggest toxic components that also contain radiation. Prevailing winds swept life away far east of washington, D.C., silencing Annapolis and points east in a widening cone of destruction. Much of the central parts of the DEL-MAR-VA peninsula are affected.

"Thus far reports of affliction have been scant as people are quickly fleeing the area, and those affected die--[choking] very suddenly. Mercifully absolutely no points in Virginia have yet been affected as the wind has maintained a steady course. I and my staff have tried repeatedly to reach someone--anyone in Maryland government, but Annapolis is silent, and we have not been able to reach the governor or his staff. We must assume the worst for the hapless representatives of Maryland.

"But there is an immediate, urgent need for me to focus on my fellow Virginians NOW. And this I will do:
First- I have called out the Virginia National Guard and supporting enforcement groups to help with rescue in Virginia along any corridors possibly affected by further fallout from this blast. Efforts are being made to set up shelters throughout central and southwest Virginia, and emergency funds and other resources, the Red Cross, Salvation Army and others are fully on board. I and my staff will personally coordinate these efforts, and let me assure you any problems will be quickly remedied.

"In the absence of a national government, let me assure you that Virginia is ready, willing and able to step up to secure her people, her borders, and to defend against any foreign threat. I have the cooperation of the Army, Navy, Marine and Air Force base commanders in the Commonwealth, and all commands are responding to my calls. Until such time as our national government can be restored, Virginia will govern these assets. Steps are already being taken to determine the nature of the threat to our citizens. Even Langley is with us! [Cheers!]

" Virginia will also open its hearts and hearths to people fleeing Maryland, and medical screening is being rushed to entry points for just this purpose.

" Second- Now let me make one thing clear: I know our national government had given over to the "pantheon of gods" philosophy. Heck, they were about to dedicate that new monument when the blast occurred.

"But in Virginia--we believe in one God- the God of Abraham, Isaac and Joseph--and we worship our Lord Jesus Christ! [wild cheers] And with Our Lord Jesus' help--and God on our side--we will overcome this great fear-- this tragedy-- and we will take on the oppressor that we have yet to name-- even if they remain anonymous.

"And so I, by act as your governor, do call upon every Virginian--and every American within the sound of my voice--to fall on your knees in prayer tonight and every evening as the sun sets, and humbly pray for those afflicted--even to forgive our enemies--and pray to the Lord Jesus Christ for our salvation that evening, night and the day to come. Thank you--good night--and may God bless you!"

Father Sperry grasped Olive's hand in the Emergency Room at St. Agnes' Hospital as he heard those words on the ER T.V. People throughout the ER were crying and shouting, "Praise Jesus!". Sperry, his eyes so full of tears and his heart so full of joy, could just make out the huge smile on Olive's patient face-- "See", she said, "I told you it is starting"!

Father Sperry knew his wife was right. THIS was the hour--THIS was the time--NOW was HOPE's finest moment--when despair seemed at its greatest power. HOPE and all the legions of Angels would rally the faithful.

Olive needed her arm and leg set. The doctors were on it at last. Sperry asked Olive if he could run a VERY important errand, and he'd be right back for her. She knew where he was going and cheered him out the door.

Sperry raced the little Corolla hard to the county lock-up. The streets were relatively bare by now- folks had either choked the highways or hunkered down at home with their T.V. sets. Seemed like an even shot at survival after all---

In the police station Father Sperry found a real mess. Cops were struggling to get all the drunks and addicts and homeless squared away. The place was overflowing with panicked people. The desk sergeant was on the phone trying to reason with a parent, and Sperry overheard the phrase: "I'm not sure yet if we are going to evacuate, so I just can't tell you!"

With a sparkle in his eye Father Sperry stepped forward and asked if he could take charge of his son. The sergeant knew the case, and with a quick phone call he was able to have the boy released under Father Sperry's recognizance. The system was looking for just such a break---

---

Erik was about to jump on the beltway to head north when he realized that it was hopelessly clogged. Even for emergency vehicles. He turned toward the back roads and passed the church they'd attended for the past few years. He saw a white Corolla in the parking lot and recognized it as Father Sperry's.

"Hell," thought Erik, "I'd better see if he's O.K." Erik wheeled into the church parking lot and told the ladies to wait for him. He entered the church sanctuary and found three figures on their knees by the prayer rail. The woman had a sling on her arm. The shadows brightened as Erik approached, and he saw Father Sperry, Olive, with a leg cast now, and their son--all holding hands and praying.

"Guys!" said Erik--" we're having a national emergency here!"
Father Sperry put his hand on Olive's shoulder and whispered something in her ear. He stood erect and, broadly smiling, walked to Erik with arms outstretched. "Join us," said Sperry- "we are in prayer".

Gene studied the skies as his flight skirted the District of Columbia. "Ladies and gentlemen-- this is your captain speaking--you no doubt are aware by now that our nation's capital was bombed today. Airports are closed, and all flights have been rerouted to other cities. We have been redirected to land in Charlotte. Please bear with us as we try to get direction on how to proceed from there. Thank you, and stand by for further updates". Cold. Clinical. Suddenly--mad texting from almost every seat in the plane.

Gene grabbed his laptop--under FILES FOR PUBLICATION he titled his article: "Religious Right's Last Straw"-- He began: "Unable to engage in rational discourse or to dispute challenges to their monolithic thinking, the religious right today threw the ultimate insult at civilization: destruction of a great symbol of hope-- our pantheon--our seat of government--our nation's library, museums, the Mall--and countless people engaged in the work of broadcasting that light of civilization. Our pantheon alone, dedicated to the proposition that all religions--like all men and women-- are created equal--was the pinnacle of centuries of struggle for world peace. Even atheists had a seat at the table. Now the shattered symbol of all humankind's work to overcome superstitions and hatred has been laid waste, smoldering before us. This is a dark day. A day of dark triumph for the Christian barbarians who would have us crusading again against our Muslim brothers and sisters, and who would leave our world in turmoil so that their CHRIST ALONE would be praised! A hollow victory for them, I can assure you. For the 21st century enlightenment will not bow to the glowering hoards of angry monotheists! We will have our Day!".

The commercial jet banked south, and no word was heard among the passengers. Stiff in his resolve, Gene silently rebuked the religion of his birth and childhood. He thought to himself, "If there WAS a Satan I'd have to congratulate him for a singular victory today; battle-lines have been drawn. And the Christians will lose".

Enlightenment meant to Gene that religions -- all religions-- past and present--are like myths of heroic tales with tragedy and triumph perfectly marking in prose man's rise out of darkness into civilization. Surely the pantheon was the next-to-final step before elevating man above all myths and supernatural longings. How close we have come, thought Gene, to the pinnacle of rational existence. So close to dispensing with tales of angels and demons and fears of things that go bump in the night. So close to elevating humanity above their gods--their superstitions --their need to separate themselves from other people to feel safe and complete. How sad, how shameful, thought Gene--that Christians can only elevate Christ through this dark deed!

Satan smiled.

Josi raptly listened to the radio at her desk in her new full-time job. The Mall in Washington obliterated? In between phone calls from desperate parents Josi wondered aloud, "What kind of God would allow this? First my boy, and now my hometown!" It seemed like she just couldn't catch a break-- too much trouble--too little energy---too little money---people at war-- leadership gone--where was HOPE? Josi busied herself at her job hoping the distraction alone would soothe her. "God, where are you?" she pled.

Arpert pulled the car door shut catching his loose tie in the door jam and jerking his neck back as he reached toward his seat belt. "Dammit! That figures--can't even get in the car anymore!" His right knee throbbed from the failed surgeries. Years of soccer and coaching--using his joints as superhuman shock-absorbers-- had finally taken out his knee. So painful and frozen. So easy to snap the wrong way. God, it hurt!

But not nearly so bad as his ego was hurt. "What the HELL's the point?" he wondered aloud. With his kids still in college and bills mounting, Arpert felt the sting of forced retirement. Sure his TIAA CREF may work out--but he'd
never be able to keep up, he was sure. "Kids all want only the best, and I can't provide for them!"

Arpert wondered about God. He wondered about prayer. He'd seen Christ's face in many a good man in his time--where was He now?

The news about the Mall in Washington barely raised an eyebrow with Arpert. "Let those bastards explain all this to those kids! They won't find it in their powerpoint presentations, now will they?!" Smug satisfaction at the irony crept across Arpert's conscious logic: THEY'LL MISS ME NOW.

Erik took Father Sperry aside in the dimly-lit chapel and said, "What's the deal? We are at WAR! This place is in trouble--let's get out of here!"

Sperry lifted his tired, sad eyes up to Erik's and with a crease of joy gave a wink--"we'd be dead by now if the winds were different-- now we are called to remain--and be a beacon". Erik was still panting and asked what Father Sperry meant.

"Olive had a vision--a vision that this place would become a beacon of light to brighten the way to Christ once again". With that, Sperry turned, gestured to the prayer altar and invited Erik and his family to join them. The ladies had already come inside.

As if Providence had spoken, Erik's daughter jerked her arm down in frustration. The cell phone would no longer send or receive texts. Erik's wife took her knowingly by the shoulders and said to Erik, "Let's follow Father Sperry".

Hope entered Erik's heart just then--for the first time in years. As if the pain were lifted, he walked with his family effortlessly to the altar--and knelt as if to pray. He clasped his hands together--looked to the right to see Sperry's family with eyes clamped shut and with broad smiles on their faces lifted up to God. Erik looked to his left and saw his wife, holding their daughter, looking imploringly at the cross on the altar, reciting the Lord's Prayer.

Erik studied his hands--sun-burnt--weather-beaten--etched with time as if old tree trunks gnarled out of his hands gripping one another--as if bracing for some great storm. Storm, yeah, that's apt--another of life's storms. Will this one have a better ending? Erik closed his eyes and arched his mind to the heavens imploring God to make this somehow DIFFERENT-- different than all the prayers before--different than all the self-serving supplications--different than the saddening results he'd seen before. His HEART was ready. And he prayed to bring Jesus RIGHT THEN--RIGHT THERE in among them all and touch them.

Just then the two ancient church doors creaked open, and a group of tentative, broken, shaggy men and women started inside. They came down the aisle to the front of the church and began to kneel facing the altar. Father Sperry jumped up and greeted them warmly, "come gather with us in the prayer chapel". The toothless man in front said, "We can't be over there with you--we are dirty and we smell". Sperry knelt in front of him, looked him square in the eyes, and pulled him into his embrace sobbing--"No man is unfit before the Grace of our Lord, Jesus Christ!" He held him close, and begged the homeless man to pray with him: "Our Father, who art in heaven, hallowed be THY NAME!"…..

Erik looked upon this sight then gazed up to see the darkened church filling with homeless, wandering, stunned people! As if on cue--they filed into the pews and dropped to their knees with their eyes lifted heavenward. A miracle?

As if a single, clear, commanding voice rang out all eyes turned toward the altar, and heads swiveled quickly as well. Tears started rolling down the faces of the gathered throng while smiles and choked "Halleluiahs!" began to flourish like an irresistible tide. What so grasped the group of shabby, exhausted and frightened people had the authority of eternity. Weeping for joy, Father Sperry giddily cried, "Praise Jesus!"

The homeless, once sick, broken and discouraged, now beamed with pride and hale and hearty laughter as they touched their arms, legs and faces. Pain and disabilities were gone! Old and crippled people stood tall and eyed each other with wonder. A mass healing had occurred…..

You see Olive had had a vision when she heard of the bombing in D.C.: she saw a joyous throng gathered in her church being healed and praising God as she and her family prayed. NOW Olive stood tall with her healed limbs strong! Tearfully she thanked God for this GREAT DAY! All were smiling and pain-free.

Lightening flashed outside the windows of Gene's jet. The plane rocked and pitched. The captain got on the loudspeaker and started to try to calm the terribly alarmed passengers and crew. With a sudden flash the speakers went dead--the cabin went black--the engines quit--and the great jet began to plunge into the rogue storm. Gene paled and hung on for dear life as he stared in fear out the plane's window. A green glow appeared out of the miasma--a glow that seemed to take shape--like a face--like eyes gleaming in pride with an evil grim forming. What terror! A pre-death hallucination? And silence.

-22-

Josi was huddled over a steaming cup of coffee worrying about the streaked windows between her and her front yard. Alone with her thoughts she struggled with trying to pray. The old sayings just fell flat. "What's wrong with me? But what's the point?" God had once again lapsed into an abstraction, especially with all the pressure Josi was under. Her church had been calling her asking if she could come to church to join them in prayer. She was avoiding the calls. Josi had too much on her plate as it was-- "Those people are too needy", she reasoned. She tried to focus: GOT to make money--GOT to take care of the kids--GOT to help her husband who's laid off--WHAT to do?!

-23-

Gene was aware of only two things: that he was no longer flying, and that he was not dead to his senses. Around him he perceived a swamp of noise, of smell, of dim, gritty shafts of light; and his flesh crawled in fear. What to make of it? Was there life in him? He could touch, but he dared not. What did he hear--voices? He was terrified at discerning their meaning. The smell--not smoke--not rotting flesh--not sweet but sour--did not beckon recognition. Above all Gene was in denial--of everything that confronted him. Was he still corporeal? What would be next? Did he dare take charge here as he had all his triumphant life--or did he think to lay low and hide out in case of a terror forthcoming? Executive skills escaped his haunted, hunted soul.

-24-

Arpert's cellphone buzzed. Buzzed in his pocket. Normally he ignored the annoyance, but his new buoyancy prompted him to fish for it.

"Hello?" "Arpert? It's Paul--Paul Lehrman--Arpert can you hear me?" Paul Lehrman, once Arpert's friend, partner and co-conspirator in the teaching business was the one man INSTRUMENTAL in Arpert's dismissal. Paul was the head of the middle school of this most prestigious private school--and Arpert hadn't fit the mold of a sleek, tech-savvy power point instructor now in demand for some time.

"What is it, Paul?", Arpert graveled lowly.

"Arpert, listen to me--the parents are tearing up the phone-lines--they want to know what Arpert Jones is saying to the kids about all this!"

"About WHAT, Paul?", Arpert poked.

"About the bombing of the Mall in D.C., about the missing leadership, the disappearing military, the church, parenting in this crisis, the school's position--my GOD, man--they demand answers!", screeched Paul.

"And what have you told them, Paul?", leveled Arpert. Arpert picked up speed and headed for home.

" I said YOU'd be making a statement at 3:00 p.m."

" I guess you lied, Paul--imagine that", smirked Arpert.

"Look, Arpert, can we put this behind us for now? With the whole school clamoring for Arpert Jones, I need you at the assembly!"

"Are you trying to piss on my dead body, Paul?" Arpert realized that his onetime friend had morphed into a bureaucratic puppet--a spin machine-- capable only limited directional thinking, and Arpert's metaphor would not even register--

"Arpert, really-- we need your body over here NOW!"

"Paul, maybe you should have considered this months ago…."

"Look, Arpert, I could apologize, but NO one saw this coming. Yesterday-- who knew? Today you are the man with the message--" "please!"

Against his better judgement, Arpert made a U-turn.

Josi's focus was on staying busy. Only thus could she avoid facing the headlines--only thus could she avoid facing the bills---only thus could she muster the energy to get up, get dressed, get to work. Work protected her-- busy she had an identity. And it felt so good to finally turn that page in her persona since her son hanged himself. Now she didn't NEED the church that she still secretly blamed. With an identity Josi would finally start to sense the tectonic rage that moved within her. She would find its VOICE.

Coming in fast now, the church was packed with crying, searching, terrified wanderers at the entrance and dancing, laughing, praising worshippers within. Like witnessing the human wave at a football stadium, the sea- change in people moving through that front door was more than electric; it was atomic. Everything changed in a wave of recognition, of sudden release from pain, from fear, from sickness, from doubt. What held the crowd at the altar transfixed pulsed to the rear of the church and acted as a beacon to the community beyond the building. Irresistible strength pulled people forth from out of their homes--to the grounds and through the doors. Nothing could keep people from slipping inside--there seemed to be room for everyone--and it just didn't stop!

Gene, aware that his wits could not serve him, tried to evade, anticipate and move to find an exit--ANY exit. The dread and oppressive atmosphere grew heavier with every sound--every breath. He could no longer describe color or smell, yet his senses were acute. Every sensation meant fear. Gene had never been so afraid in his life--was he alive?

Arpert pulled into the familiar school driveway, usually vacant at this hour . But this time Paul stood clearly by Arpert's old parking spot. Arpert parked, stepped out of the car. Paul smiled and extended his hand-- Arpert looked Paul in the eye without taking his hand and asked, "What now?"

Paul apologized--"I would not have called you if it weren't important".

"You mean you're in trouble", cut in Arpert.

"I mean there are some families in very high places that want their kids to hear from Arpert Jones".

"Did you tell them you let me go?"

"Of course not! I said you were on your way out of town, and we would plead with you to return and speak to the school assembly--at least I told a partial truth."

"And did you tell them I was going to be around after that?"

"I said you were a most-prized Master".

"That used to be true", dismissed Arpert.

Paul escorted Arpert to the assembly of combined middle and upper schools-- and all the faculty, administration --and many parents were huddled in attendance. Cameras and cell phones began to click as Arpert made his way through cheering lads eleven to eighteen years of age. The headmaster, surrounded by the school board, was grinning foolishly as he nodded admiringly at Arpert for the sake of his image at this moment in time. He stepped to Arpert's inclined ear and very quietly and urgently said, "The truth is, Arpert, you probably always knew what you were talking about--and today these kids-- we all--need to hear the truth". Arpert's shoulders slumped. What an ass, he thought.

Arpert stepped to the podium, tapped the microphone, and to uproarious cheers, raised his hand in an attempt to calm the gathering.

"Good morning", said Arpert, although it was late. "Good morning, at last we are AWAKE!" Cheers of approval seared the air. The boys in the middle school were always attuned to Arpert Jones' sardonic approach to the truth.

"We apparently have awakened, as a nation, to a new truth--about ourselves! The explosion on the Mall and the deadly cloud that has since killed everyone in its path has marched right into our very souls. A great mirror has been shoved in our national face-- and our leaders have shrunk from it!"

You could hear a pin drop. Arpert did not look to Paul, the headmaster or

anyone in authority for approval. He looked right into the eyes of the
pupils. They hungered for the truth.

"We've grown accustomed to some all-too-convenient 'TRUTHS'", Arpert
started, "and we've left the rest of the story just as conveniently untold.
Challenges to our approved-of history lessons have been met with scorn and
denial. One wonders how democracy can survive with the truth only half
illuminated and the rest suppressed.

" Just as a third of our nation was disgraced, and its own stories and
truths suppressed after the War Between the States, so too were the truths
about every unpopular minority suppressed in American until their own day
of reckoning.

"Today we witness a day of reckoning for Constitutionalists and Christians
all across this great land. For too long you've worshipped at the altar of
political correctness", [contagious cheering][pause] "and the inherent
weakness in moral relativism brought our great nation to its knees. Your
elected leaders largely sought political inertness in order to avoid
criticism from the politically correct moral relativists. They honed their
skills at sounding passionate about NOTHING! Our legislation, legal
proceedings, even worship and classroom teaching became relativistic
poison! And you, the students, were the wisest among us, challenging this
empty hoax.

"An architectural marvel stands hollow and empty on the Mall today, that
Pantheon, that National place of worship to NOTHING, stands empty while
poison still clutches the ground. That poison came as a first call: people
with different principles, different beliefs, and a whole lot of hate for
our despised way of life are headed this way." [crowd booing]

"Just because our leadership is morally irrelevant and incapable of
organizing a response from their position of relativism, remember some
Americans still STAND on the firm principles of our founding
fathers!" [wild cheers]

"For one, the governor of Virginia has issued a decree uniting Virginians
and all who need to follow under his firm constitutionally-based
leadership. He has given credit to Our Lord and Savior, Jesus Christ
[cheering and shouts of approval], and he plans to stem the tide of this
catastrophe under that banner! [cheers]

"This was once a Christian school [now looking at the headmaster and his
minions] and, by God, it can be again! [wild cheering]
Follow Christ's teachings, follow our own United States Constitution--never
suppress the truth--and we can overcome ANYTHING!"

Amid shouts of approval and cheering in every octave of the human voice,
Arpert waved and headed for the exit. He was mobbed by students lifting him
up and chanting: "Mr. J for President! Mr. J for President!"

Gene groped in the stench and terror until he felt his chest. He slipped
his hand in his shirt to see if he could still feel a heart beat. And as he
did, the cross he wore around his neck, a golden ornament given him by his

wife, slipped between his fingers. He felt the metal, he felt the image in his mind--and the irony did not escape him.

What if? --thought Gene--what IF Jesus was REAL? As if his very thoughts were broadcast, a deep, taunting chuckle came from everywhere!

Casting about, Gene searched for a way--ANY way--away from this terrifying place. On his hands and knees with his head low to avoid detection, he scraped across the gritty floor--to what? Gene's hands came across a smooth surface--his arms stretched out to feel an outline--a stone slab--smooth on the edges and polished on the surface--no--wait--there were indentations in lines--words--letters!

Gene pulled himself up and traced blindly the lines of letters until he found their top. Slowly he wiped away the grit, and half-feeling--half seeing --he made out the following:

THE NOISY PRETENDERS TO EXCLUSIVE HUMANITY WITH REFINED TASTES AND QUIVERING MORALITY, BREATHING AND SOARING ABOVE INSTITUTIONALIZED THINGS LIKE CHURCHES AND STATES- THEY KNOW BETTER.

"Need a clearer mirror than that?" hissed the serpentine voice nearby.

"Think Thomas Jefferson saw you coming lo, those many years ago?" bellowed a beast!

"Like this final resting place? You're not alone, deary!" whined a siren-like female.

Shaking so hard his hands were pounding the stone, Gene muttered, "What?"

"HAVE YOU FORGOTTEN ALL YOUR PRONOUNCEMENTS---KNOWING YOU WERE SMARTER? KNOWING YOU HAD TRUMPED EVEN GOD?!"

The creature loomed everywhere--outside him--trying to invade his very brain.

"I may have misspoken…" trailed Gene.

"LIAR! POLITICIAN! PATRICIAN! SCOUNDREL!" Roaring laughter from all voices previously heard now in unison saying, "YOU BELONG TO ME! I AM READY FOR YOU!"

Gene cried bitterly, knowing deep within he had philosophized, bartered and wheedled away the essence of his faith and replaced it with his own, well-rehearsed, well-groomed, self-serving dissertations.

Choking for air--tears flowing now like a child's, Gene grasped the cross about his neck.

THEY'LL NEVER GET THIS! vowed Gene to himself. With no words left to speak--with no thoughts worthy of his pain--Gene gripped the cross and dug it deep into his hand. THIS MUST NOT GO--I MUST DIE WITH CHRIST IN ME EVEN IF NO ONE CAN SEE!

"DESIST! thundered the atmosphere, and with that Gene felt himself thrown upward and dropped like a stone.

Shattering pain. No way to breathe.

And then--brilliance--light blinding him suddenly--pierced the storm of terror.

Gene, suddenly calm, witnessed the light divide the terrible place, and, like the purest of surgeries reached down to bathe him--and only him, in its brilliance.

"Will you follow me?" heard Gene.

That voice, so sure, so strong, so loving and inviting--he looked up and saw the face: The SON Himself--reaching down with an outstretched hand--pierced from his own crucifixion yet totally whole--PURE LOVE--NO being more perfect-- coming for him!

As worthless as he felt, Gene reached up with the hand imbedded with the gold cross--Christ held it--examined it--smiled into Gene's eyes and lit up his heart. "Better late than never, eh?"

Sobbing with the purest joy--that greatest thanks--Gene grasped his God--His Christ--His Jesus with both arms and cried, "I am not worthy! I promise you!"

Jesus looked into Gene's eyes--through his heart into his living soul.

"You have chosen ME".

                                   -30-

The governor of Virginia looked grim as he placed the phone back in its cradle on his desk in Richmond.

"What is it, sir?" asked his aide.

"General Petrarch has landed and is setting up shop in the Pentagon".

"And what did he say, sir?"

"He is summoning--HIS words--all the governors to meet with him in his press room tomorrow", said the governor in a flat voice.

"Sir, you don't think.." trailed the aide.

"It's my greatest fear, Don--rumors have it he has already pinned a 5th star on himself--he already put McCrimmon back in charge in the Middle East, and now he's made himself--with no civilian authorization---full general over all the combined armed forces."

"Sir, this could be disastrous."

"Don, will you pray with me?"

"Yes, sir." And the two men stood as equals in the sight of God.

"Lord Jesus, Don and I just received what may be the second most dangerous news this week after the destruction of our civilian national government. Please, Lord God, hold us, KEEP us, and hold our PEOPLE safe from any corruption or any further violence…….Don?"

"Yes, God, please help us in this terrible time--and please guide all of us here to do your will and feed your sheep".

And together they said, "AMEN!"

The phone rang again--"Sir, it's the director of the CIA".

"Please put him through."

"Good morning, Director--yes, I got the call--General Petrarch wants us all there at 0900 tomorrow sharp--you too? And the FBI? Regional Directors as well I take it? ALL the surviving directors and Regional Directors of all government agencies? OK, then. I guess he's not asking for an intimate gathering then, is he? And surviving Congressmen? I guess he wants a good head count of his own then? Well this might get interesting. Yes, I still maintain civilian authority here. You can count on that. OK then, I look forward to seeing you then. Be safe, and God Speed."

With that, for a second time in this hour, the Virginia governor gravely placed the phone back on its cradle on his desk.

"Don, the CIA Director shares my concern it would seem--he thinks General Petrarch will attempt some kind of coup".

Don went ashen.

NEXT DAY: 0900 PENTAGON PRESS ROOM: "THIS IS FOX NEWS LIVE from the Pentagon where you've heard General Petrarch is holding a briefing, broadcast live, for all the combined U.S. government authorities: agency heads and Regional Directors and the states' governors. Apparently the general is wearing 5 stars now--no general has worn 5 stars since Omar Bradley. And it's not clear who would have conferred on him that distinction--we are waiting for the general to take the podium. There seems to be some lively side-talk among the governors gathered here. It would appear that none of them were briefed on what the general is about to say-- and the mood here is one of concern--yes, almost worry--about what General Petrarch might say. And here he comes now….."

The general's aide walks to the microphone and shouts:" Ladies and Gentlemen--General Petrarch!" [polite applause]

With the general taking the podium, a company of desert-cammo-clad troops entered the room, carrying M-16 rifles, and fanned out surrounding the throng. An audible gasp erupted in many sections, and the room fell silent.

"Ladies and Gentlemen", smiled Petrarch--"distinguished governors, directors, regional directors, Senators and Members of the House--I am glad you survived!" The general stood there with a great smile on his face and his hands outstretched as if open to a warm cheer to follow his opening words. Instead he got a trickle of nervous laughter.

" I return to this tragic scene here at home with at least some good news from abroad: The Middle East is secure!" [again silence]

" I have put General McCrimmon back in charge over there so I could come put things in order here at home. The heads of state in Europe, Asia and the Middle East have each personally assured me their fullest cooperation through this national crisis. In the absence of the Joint Chiefs and our beloved Executives and the Cabinet, and with the death of the Speaker of the House, the President Pro Tempore of the Senate, and other ranking members of Congress, I have assumed emergency authority with the aim of protecting the American people and providing essential services. I have secured all nuclear platforms and maintain full control of their capability". [again a huge, solicitous smile with outstretched arms seeking approval. Nothing came.]

"To help me in this I have asked the surviving commands of the armed services to join me--and no one has yet objected--and now I ask each of you today--with the American people as our witness--to join me in bringing order quickly to our great land".

"Each of you present--to help ensure your safety and to facilitate communication with my command--will be assigned a squadron guard for your round-the-clock protection. They will eat, sleep and move about with you and your families".

"Today I am instituting martial law with price-fixing and a curfew at sunset. Rationing of vital goods and supplies will commence as soon as a system for coupon distribution can be arranged. Other measures to ensure public safety will be announced as needs arise. Until this national emergency has passed, and until we can see an orderly transition of national authority--I am assuming emergency powers".

A lone hand waves from the governors' gaggle.

"The governor of Virginia is recognized".

"General, by what--by whose authority to take these sweeping measures do you so decree?"

"Governor, history dictates to us that when there is a power vacuum, someone will rise to fill it. Just as Abraham Lincoln took emergency measures to preserve the UNION --so now do I assume the responsibility to steer our crippled nation forward".

"General, Abraham Lincoln, though usurping constitutional authority in his own time, was at least a duly-elected official".

"Governor, all our duly-elected leaders in the chain of executive succession are dead or missing to my knowledge, and until the People of the United States can safely hold a new election I will not sleep or shrink from my duty".

Petrarch continued: "But to help ease us toward that election day I will appoint an advisory council from among this body of surviving elected officials here with us today", added General Petrarch.

"And how will you choose said council?" asked Virginia's governor.

" I will select twelve advisors based on their talents and expertise needed to help me--the American people--- through this great emergency," answered Petrarch.

"Thank you--I have an important meeting now with the new Russian ambassador who just arrived here today. Ladies and Gentlemen--the American people--God Bless America!" And with that, General Petrarch took his leave of the hall. With murmuring in the crowd, the soldiers stood firmly at attention.

FOX NEWS INTERJECTED: " And there you have it--the general has spoken-- martial law until further notice, and I'm not certain everyone here is in agreement. Turning now to our Chief Political Correspondent, Brit Hume-- Brit, what is your take on what we just heard here today?"

Brit appeared, red-faced and began: "I confess, Steve, I am a little startled by this announcement by General Petrarch--as far as I know there is no Constitutional precedent for his actions--and the Supreme Court members are all deceased--I think we are witnessing something entirely new here---"

Suddenly the anchor broke in--"Brit, I have to turn our attention now to the group of governors still assembled here--they are motioning to each other to gather round--let me see if we can get a statement. Excuse me, sirs--Steve Hartzel from Fox News --- can you tell me how the governors plan to coordinate with General Petrarch?"

"Steve", injected the Governor of Virginia, "we are gathering here as American governors to talk over the implications of what we heard here today. We will have to get back to you with a statement". With that the governors pulled together again, heatedly.

"Gentlemen and Ladies", started the Virginia governor, "we are still missing the governor from Maryland, but I believe we should convene quickly to define our positions, as States, and do so quickly before we are too- closely baby-sat".

Suddenly the CIA Director poked his head in--

"Folks, I have to tell you--I am lost--I was appointed by the President of the United States, and I am not authorized to serve under an army general".

"Director", said the Virginia governor," I cannot speak for my fellow governors, but I find myself in a similar dilemma. If you want my advise, stay close to the Constitution and your Code of Ethics. We will contact you personally when we have reached a position--THANK you."

The governors decided to adjourn and reconvene in the ancient governor's palace in Williamsburg, Virginia that afternoon at 5:00 p.m. They would have to act fast.

Shooting down Interstate -95 in the governor's limo, the Virginia governor hung up the phone after arranging the governor's palace meeting.

"Dan, we have a Constitutional crisis on our hands, and I don't know how we are going to handle this"---[thinking out loud]--"on the one hand General Petrarch's help could really be valuable in keeping foreign powers in cooperation with our national interests. But, he is not Constitutionally empowered to step back on these shores and take over! From my perspective it is the authority of the individual sovereign states--with the help of their Guard forces--to ensure their safety within their own borders. Once state representatives can be chosen to convene again in Congress at a safe place--then and only then will we have a legitimate national authority to deal with. It's a puzzle what to do with Petrarch".

Dan interjected:" Is he willing to work with you, governor?--It doesn't seem so".

"On his terms only it would seem--that's why I think we governors all should try to speak to him with one voice".

-33-

Josi's school called. The principal was breathless--"Josi, how are your skills at note-taking?"

"I did graduate from William and Mary with a major in English--pretty good, I'd say", said Josi.

"That's what I told the superintendent. She called looking for a smart, skilled wordsmith/secretary with an ear for HISTORY. You immediately came to mind!"

"Me? Why?" asked Josi.

"Your intelligence, wisdom, and faith in God were specifically asked for--AND you went to W&M", noted the principal.

"Why is W&M significant?"

"Because the combined governors of the United States are being hosted by our Virginia governor in emergency session ---the superintendent said it's going to be an historic occasion, and they want someone to take minutes--like a court note-taker--but with authority, a sense of history, style and discretion. And William and Mary is the governor's alma mater."

"Uh, when do I have to be there? And where do I go?" asked Josi.

"By 3:00 p.m. today--you pretty much need to leave now--can they send the car? The governor's assistant will have to brief you along the way."

"Sure--give me 30 minutes to get dressed. Thanks. Bye".

Josi put the phone down, wrote a note to her boys and husband and hit the closet.

Dan, the governor's assistant pulled up out front of Josi's home with a driver. He hopped out, and seeing Josi emerge from her house, opened the car door as if for a dignitary.

"Hi, I'm Dan--the governor's personal assistant." Virginia was all over this vehicle from the plates to the Sic Semper Tyrannis lettering on the door.

"Hi, I'm Josi, and I guess you have something to tell me."

On the fast, escorted trip down Shirley Highway Dan started the story:

"Josi, you've come highly recommended..the governor of Virginia needs a Christian patriot---a wordsmith with great secretarial skills and with a deep appreciation for history-in-the-making. And with your W&M background all fingers pointed to you! Your discretion in keeping confidential what you record here is essential. Are you up for this? There will be some long days ahead."

"If I knew what you were talking about, maybe", retorted Josi in her usual style.

"Well", said Dan wryly, "soon enough. Welcome aboard!"

The limousine sped toward Williamsburg with blue State Police lights flashing forward and aft.

At 5:00 p.m. sharp the Governor of Virginia stepped up to the podium and calmed the small gathering. "Fellow governors--will you please join me in the Pledge of Allegiance and a brief prayer?" After some murmuring all rose, saluted or covered their hearts and recited the pledge.

Virginia's governor then intoned: "Heavenly Father, we gather here today as humble servants--humble elected heads of our several sovereign states--knowing our weakness and fallibility--imploring your mercy and guidance in facing not only the problems of our own states, but the urgent governing crisis of our combined United States. Lord, in your mercy, hear our prayer! In Jesus Precious Name, AMEN!" The gathering roared the last without exception.

"Now I know not every one of you here is Christian, but most of us serve constituencies that are largely Christian. I ask we not overlook that detail in our work here today. I call upon my God in times like these, and I do not try to hide this from my fellow Virginians for the sake of political expediency [several "hear-hear's"]. I ask that you invoke your God publicly --to lift our united peoples from despair into hope.

"I asked you here because we were close-by this morning at the Pentagon and because some of our earliest representatives struggled in this very city to carve out the essentials of American democracy. We are meeting in the colonial governor's palace, well, because we're governors, and because I'm terribly proud of this heritage. It's time, I believe, to save that very effort our forefathers put forth---from destruction.

"Now we have no evidence yet that the Executive and Judicial branches in Washington were wholly destroyed--we believe so, but we haven't solid proof yet. The same goes for the majority of our nation's legislative branch. A few, we've seen this morning, were fortunate enough to have been away from Congress during the blast. The rest may well be gone.

"But what we've seen today is the first spasmodic attempt to unite all Americans under one voice--for better or for worse. Now I've never known General Petrarch to disobey orders. But today he has no formal boss, save the American people, and he seems determined to lead rather than follow. He nailed that point. [moaning]

"This leaves us governors with some tough decisions and choices to make. First in my mind, and I want your views on these please, do we tell General Petrarch how we feel about all this? Second, what is our actual position in light of our constitutional covenant with the U.S. government, and third, what are we prepared to do?"

Josi's eyes were as big as saucers as she played the scribe. There she was: almost center stage in American politics, writing down HISTORY!

"With that", continued Virginia's governor, "I propose that we follow our several state constitutions in discussing our obligation to lead. Now let me point out a piece of irony here: worst-case scenario, and we have to bolt from some national dictator's grasp. Virginia and most of the southern states who joined the Confederacy in 1860-61, let me remind you, were not accepted back into the United States fold after the war until they had new state constitutions that forbade their states from ever seceding again.

" So according to our southern constitutions, not your northern ones, we are obligated to remain with the Union come what may! [northern governors chuckle nervously].

"Now we all can see in light of today's misgivings how arbitrary and undemocratic this detail becomes! [general laughter]

" I am not proposing disunion, my brothers and sisters! If anything we owe the American people a united stand to preserve the freedoms and the very constitutional government that used to guarantee those freedoms! [cheers]

"So let me open to this important, historic gathering a call for statements, positions and suggestions".

The governor of California raised a hand--"Governor, although we live on the opposite coast from all this mess, let me assure you we feel the full effect--our federal funding is now defunct!" [laughter--coughing]

"I believe we need to act firmly to secure the interests of our own people and also reach out to help our sister states in need as the federal government appears to be foundering. [shouts of approval] And we need to prepare state by state to send new representatives to form a new Congress in Washington. I caution, however, against allowing a general to call the shots as Chief Executive, or whatever he may call himself, until such time as elections are held to replace our national government. I say we operate independently until we can restart the political process nationally on a truly representative basis!" [cheers]

The governor of Texas raised a hand and added," I agree with my esteemed friend from California--but I want to add that we need to secure our borders, and I propose that we call upon our Guard units to do so under our executive authority as governors. We may even have to recruit militia under the auspices of our county sherifs. The good governor of Virginia has already accomplished this to great effect, and I would like to duplicate his success as we have an international border to consider".

Pennsylvania's governor raised his hand and said, "Now we also may need to choke off this usurper, Petrarch, before he gets to full of himself. [silence in the hall] I hope we are all agreed that he has exceeded his authority, and we need to cut his lifeline, and he must lay down!" [voices of approval and some applause]

The governor of Michigan added, "And we have to shut down the U.S. military until it can be brought back under civil authority--but how?"

"This is the question of the hour it would seem, ladies and gentlemen", said Virginia's governor--"How?"

Josi knew the moment she'd heard of the explosion on the Mall that havoc would sweep their lives, but she had no clue she would be privy to such great undertakings! Humbly she lowered her head and quickly asked God to invest every heart and mind in this humble gathering.

Father Sperry was used to being the one who did all the talking in his sanctuary, but this certainly was NOT his show! As if years of prayer, praising, encouraging and shepherding had suddenly bloomed in exultant abundance, Sperry just stood there, humbled and transfixed with a smile that wouldn't quit. He feasted his eyes on the Miracle of the Saved, as he might call it, hundreds and hundreds of souls gathered praising Jesus with song, dance, waving arms, hugging, crying, searching heavenward, marveling in the lights in each others' eyes! Seamless joy--seamless praise--complete, wildly complete.

Father Sperry's son reached up, tugged on his father's shoulder and whispered loudly, "Dad, I just couldn't even imagine--THANK YOU!"

Erik's daughter, too, spoke up: "Finally, something better than VH-1!" Erik turned stunned with the notion that she might have really missed something here--but he was suddenly thrilled to see in his daughter's face and eyes the rapture of the moment--she still managed a sardonic humorous quip in the process! He threw his arms around her in deepest love. Jesus had swept through them all! Erik's wife was huddled in prayer with Olive, tearfully waving her arms skyward. Erik was never so hopeful--never so full--never so thankful!

Arpert opened the squeaky car door ready to shake the dust from his feet at that school once and for all. Sure his kids carried him out of the hall and waved him off with cheers. Arpert didn't think the administration would be thankful for any of it. Too many times Arpert had made bold declarations of truth the way he saw it ---only to be put under investigation or charged with failing to respond to his supervisor's e-mails in a timely fashion. God forbid a parent should complain--that often brought the politically-correct police down on him. Arpert remembered a time when lively debate of issues was the stuff of great minds--and instilling the art of critical thinking was a treasured part of teaching. He also remembered bitterly the time he brought a Civil War -era-rifle into the class to demonstrate how technology had changed from flintlock smoothbore to cap and ball rifle with an effective range that could drive off enemy artillery! Arpert was nearly brought up on a charge. Education was little more than regurgitation and pleasing anymore. Challenge to think and imagine was dead. These kids today were doomed to lives of following in a manner not too dissimilar from the Hitler Youth.

Arpert was pulling out of the parking spot when Paul jumped out of nowhere and beat on the hood of Arpert's car. He motioned for Arpert to roll down the driver's-side window.

"Arpert--that was pretty plucky in there---I don't know where you come up with some of that stuff--and I don't know that I agree with you--but it's red meat for the hungry crowd up there! We want you back!" Paul had his hand outstretched to shake Arpert's.

Arpert looked into Paul's eyes--there used to be a soul in there-- Arpert could remember it--now he's just a machine---"Uh, Paul, no thanks, you can buy two kids out of college for what you pay me, and they won't give you any trouble."

"Come on, Arpert! For old times' sake…"

"Frankly I'm just not interested anymore", Arpert lied, choking back tears. With that he just drove away.

Father Sperry wasn't even aware of the fact that day had become night. The worshippers kept flooding in, and people were praising and praying and holding each other-- witnessing all they'd seen and felt. No one showed hunger, thirst or fatigue. No stress or timetable threatened. If Sperry didn't know better, he'd say they were all standing on the brink of heaven!

Just as Father Sperry was about to embrace his wife again, a loudspeaker outside broke the mood.

"YOU ARE ORDERED TO DISPERSE! MARTIAL LAW WITH A 9:00 P.M. CURFEW IS IN EFFECT, AND YOU ARE IN VIOLATION!"

Father Sperry knew of no such regulation, but then again, he'd been off his usual diet of Fox News for many hours! Another miracle.

General Petrarch had been advised that Maryland, particularly Baltimore, in the absence of civil authority, was in chaos and would be a problem. He'd deployed every available troop and armored vehicle to the Baltimore area looking for civil unrest. The young lieutenant with this CAV unit from the nearest armored division was on patrol when he came upon the thousands mobbing the church property. He'd passed word along the ranks to advise folks to get home before the 9:00 p.m. curfew, but word came back to him quickly that no one paid it any mind, and people were encouraging troops to join in! Some did, and they could not be found again. Stunned, the lieutenant had ordered back-up and armored APC's, and two tanks were now grinding up the church lawn.

Father Sperry worked his way outside the sanctuary to be blinded by the glare of spot-lights atop humming vehicles across the 180-degrees of view. He made his way toward one light, and shielding his eyes, he asked for the man or woman in charge.

Suddenly a loudspeaker blurted: " You there! Are you in charge here?"

"Well", chuckled Sperry, "the Holy Spirit is in CHARGE here, but it is my church."

" Then order your people to disperse and return to their homes! Martial law is in effect and the curfew ordered by General Petrarch has been in effect since 9:00 p.m.".

"That's not possible", argued Sperry, "this is a spontaneous outpouring of the Holy Spirit--these people cannot be stopped!" The crowd continued to sing, praise and press toward the church door.

"Then I will have to stop this mob action as it constitutes civil unrest, according to my orders", snapped the loudspeaker.

"That's just nonsense, sir! These people --" and Sperry was abruptly stopped short when he was thrown to the ground face-first by several uniformed men. He was then cuffed painfully from behind. Old weight-lifting tendons did not give the way they used to.

Still protesting, Father Sperry was stuffed into a well-guarded armored personnel carrier and driven a half a block away. From his position in the troop carrier Sperry could still hear the loudspeaker barking orders. The crowd still swelled with songs of praise as if oblivious to the demands. Sperry was worried about the people now as his anger shifted. What if his family and the others should get roughed up in all this? How can he help them? Panic set in.

Sperry was about to raise more protest when suddenly, BAM! and BAM--BAM--BAM- BOOM! To Father Sperry's sheer terror he could swear he heard stone crumbling and glass shattering around those concussions.

After that--nothing---no cries--no shouts--no songs--not even swearing. Just the hum of military diesel engines whirring all about him. Sperry heard an astonished, indecipherable exclamation from someone outside his vehicle. What HORROR?!

"Sir", said Dan to the Virginia Governor as he leaned in during the late-night session.

"You need to hear this: According to the news General Petrarch had troops shell a large outdoor gathering at a church in suburban Baltimore. It was after the 9:00 p.m. curfew, and it was officially deemed a riotous mob scene. A large section of the mid-nineteenth-century sanctuary was destroyed. There are no known survivors." [Breathless silence].

Shocked, the Virginia governor furrowed his brow and asked," You mean every person assembled was shot to death individually?"

"Apparently not, sir. According to this the church was shelled, but hundreds died without receiving a scratch they say--it was a thoroughly shocking scene."

"Petrarch has gone too far, damn it, and we've GOT to put a stop to it! I need to speak out now."

The Virginia governor took a turn at the podium at the still-going late-night governors' meeting.

He began gravely. "Gentlemen, ladies, I've just received word that General Petrarch's command outside Baltimore shelled a church gathering deemed a mob scene by the commanding officer present. It could happen next in any one of our back yards! Not in MY back yard I'll tell you! [roaring approval]

"Now we've got to make a stand, and we've got to do it now. Josi, I need you to prepare a document for all our signatures. We've deliberated the legalities of this all evening, and we've come full circle. We can pound out the practical details afterward, but right now we have to communicate leadership to our constituencies, our people at home. We have to show Petrarch it's time for him to stand down.

"I've taken the liberty of inviting the directors of the CIA and the FBI as well as the NSA to join us here for the signing. They each have indicated their support in our attempt to reconstruct civilian authority, and they will help advise us, as governors, and our own state agencies on how to keep things running smoothly until we have elected a new national government and it has had a chance to convene to take charge. Josi, get your pen ready".

Josi was scribbling faster than she ever had, and in spite of her exhaustion from not using a computer, she was thrilled at the prospect of helping draft such a momentous document. It was only SO like the signing of the Declaration of Independence all over again! The Governor of Virginia took a stack of written statements and started, at the behest of the gathering, to dictate a draft. It sounded very much like an 18th century moment:

"KNOW ALL MEN, that we, the undersigned elected governors of our several states, do declare our States sovereign in the execution of all the peoples' business. We further declare that we will cooperate with each other in securing this sovereign authority and will duly elect representatives to convene at a future date to re-establish federal authority for the United States government. Until such a Congress can convene, all federal authority, civil and military, will revert to the civilian command of the several sovereign States as appropriate. The District of Columbia, the State of Maryland and all U.S. military and other government agencies represented abroad will fall under the authority of the Commonwealth of Virginia until such time as national and Maryland civilian control can be reestablished. All military and government agencies shall herewith report to the governors in the State where they are now established."

"What shall we call this, sir? asked Josi.

The governor of Hawaii suggested:

THE DECLARATION OF STATE SOVEREIGNTY.

"A little broad, but I like it", said the Governor of Arizona, "we've needed something like this for a long time!" [general laughter]

Josi, pleased with the document she penned, handed it up to the governors to view. Each took it, and smiled. They were pleased with the breadth and depth of it's reach, and one at a time applied their signatures as if it were a final draft.

Fox News, CNN, NBC, CBS and ABC were called to cover the breaking news.

Rocked beyond all belief, Olive and the ladies huddled in terror in the rectory long after the blasts and shouting ceased. No one dared even raise a limb near a window. Everyone lay flat and silent on the hallway floor-- silent save for their barely audible sobs and gasps for air. Erik peered up over his arms, crawled to the window facing the church--his wife protesting his foolishness---and raised up enough to look outside.

After Father Sperry had exited the church to meet with the military outside, Erik got an onerous feeling--a gut reaction with no rational explanation --a gut feeling straight from his experience in combat in the Middle East. Fear speaks from experience--often on a level too sophisticated to communicate verbally. Erik saw the pastor exit the church--glimpsed the spotlights outside----and he KNEW--he smelled--he was SHOVED into the belief that he needed to evacuate. Rather than create panic, Erik calmly gathered his loved ones and all who heard, and he gently led them out of the back of the church--through the narrow corridor of church offices---and out the back walkway to the rectory. Surprisingly no one--no worshippers--no military were in sight along that path. The small group--a mere dozen or so--made it into the rectory where Erik spoke.

"Now keep very quiet, and do not be afraid. We need to keep the lights off, and just lay down on the floor. No, no time for talk just now--TRUST me on this!"

No sooner had Erik uttered these words when a loud crack followed in rapid succession by other cracks, and explosions rocked the air. The whole frame of the house shuddered with each blast, and the women shrieked. Erik begged them to be silent and hold each other tight with their heads down. Whimpering, they obeyed.

Now Erik shook as he peered out the window into the night. Spotlights bathed the front and side of the church. Erik saw what looked like masses of people lying still on the ground--he didn't know what to make of it except that they may have gotten the message to stay flat.

Suddenly an APC started up the driveway toward the rectory with a blinding searchlight searing Erik's eyes. He dropped to the floor and told the dozen with him to lay flat and stay QUIET. The APC zoomed up the driveway-- stopped dead out front of the rectory, and with orders hollering outside, Erik heard footsteps rushing about. A couple of men topped the stairs to the porch and flashlights shone straight into the vestibule. The lights hit all the walls at waist height or higher, then turned away to the porch. Someone in charge shouted, "Clear!", and the troops bounded down the stairs. Erik was grateful for their inexperience and haste.

General Petrarch watched the FOX and CNN coverage of the governors' press release. His face reddening, he raised a fist in the air and spit,

"THIS is the HERO's welcome I get coming home to save America from chaos and terrorism?! No good deed goes unpunished!"

Having just received word of the averted criminal uprising just west of Baltimore, Petrarch felt even more justified in his sentiments.

"They can TRY to take over, but they have no authority over the U.S. military! And the military is under legitimate control--our control--chain of command--and until a new President, Joint Chiefs and Secretary of Defense are found I will not shrink from my duty!"

With this General Petrarch ordered the major east coast cities sealed, under military control. All comings and goings by land, sea and air would be subject to search and seizure, and Petrarch would ensure public order and safety. Convoys of supplies were under way, and the chain-of-command well-briefed. One order stood clear: "Any resistance to military chain-of-command shall be met with swift suppression". The type of retaliation was left to the local command, as Petrarch knew logistics would be difficult. He trusted his men and women in uniform to secure the homefront.

Josi woke suddenly to a firm pounding on the office complex door in Richmond. She'd fallen asleep trying to keep up with the comings and goings at the Virginia governor's office the night before. No one tried to disturb her rest until now.

"Open up! This is Colonel Massey with General Petrarch's command. We have orders to protect the governor."

Josi, fighting sleep, bolted upright to get to the door. There was no evidence of activity in the office complex around her.

"How may I help you?" asked Josi when she opened the door.

"Colonel Massey, M'am. Are you with the governor's office?"

"Well, I was--"

"Never mind, I need to find the governor! General Petrarch has determined that there is a threat to the governor's safety, and we've been sent to take the governor and his staff into protection".

Josi raised her hands in a legitimate gesture that showed ignorance--

"Where is the governor?!" demanded the colonel.

"I just woke up, and I don't know," said Josi.

Scowling, Massey impetuously pushed his way inside, and he was followed by a dozen troops carrying short, automatic weapons. The troops fanned out searching for staff--the governor--in every corner of every room. Josi heard the words of last night's declaration ringing in her ears as she witnessed this "protection".

"Ok, lady, what's your name, and what's your job here?" demanded Colonel Massey.

"I am NOBODY--I am a school administrative secretary called down from Reston to help with the typing pool," she mostly lied. Josi, a committed Christian, believed that this was NOT the time to offer the full truth. She'd deal with her SIN later.

"And why were you sleeping in the Virginia Governor's inner-sanctum?"

" I was so tired from yesterday that I just shut my eyes and didn't wake up until you knocked! They haven't gotten much work out of this gal, I can tell you! What's wrong? Am I in danger?"

The colonel studied Josi's face looking for a ruse, but found only worry in her face. Growing up in her world, Josi knew how to show the emotion she wanted to portray. It certainly was a useful skill in schools!

Colonel Massey decided this woman was not high enough on the food chain to detain or waste any more valuable time on. As his men cleared the area, he ordered them back outside.

"Lady, I'm not sure who you really are or what you're doing here, but you'd better get word to the governor that we've got to bring him in for his own protection". Josi could certainly see that he was lying--this man was no match for the common high-schooler!

"Yes sir!"

The colonel left and slammed the door. Josi plopped back on the couch and let out an audible sigh. Two things occurred: where was the coffee, and WHAT NOW?

Arpert had the radio tuned to talk radio as he drove up to the Korean-owned KWIKIE-MART. Diet Coke was his last addiction, and he was in no mood to give it up. The radio commentator was not sounding as cocky and condescending as was his habit; rather he sounded confused, perplexed. The conservative talk-show host presented a deep dilemma. While always pro-military in the past---this avowed Tea-Party supporter decried General Petrarch's seizing national authority under his self-proclaimed martial law. He struggled with constitutional issues, and he stated that, while he felt Petrarch had his heart in the right place, he was sure Petrarch had lost his head.

Arpert smiled a knowing smile: ABSOLUTE POWER CORRUPTS ABSOLUTELY. Not so hard to comprehend. Without constitutional checks and balances any person in charge could overcompensate trying to face a national threat. Arpert had studied countless good-hearted men through history who had done this. While it was rare in a democracy--emergency situations brought some notables close to tyranny until they'd had their sails trimmed. Sadly, as in the case of Abe Lincoln, assassination was one cure. Arpert recalled great reports on general Petrarch and his work abroad. He hoped it would never come to that in his case.

Arpert got his Diet Coke and jumped back into his car. With army trucks and armored personnel carriers no longer surprising on local roads, he wondered what would come of Virginia's governor and his staff.

Maryland's governor and staff were still apparently missing--a real strange occurrence as folks speculated he was hiding north somewhere now that he lost everything. But the combined governors really took a stand with their joint declaration, thought Arpert, and he hadn't heard of General Petrarch reporting for duty to the Virginia governor. He feared the worst: a civil struggle that could get bloody. And worse yet: what would the net political result do to America? The terrorists who detonated the dirty bomb no doubt hoped for the worst.

Arpert had a hunch: he figured the military would try to "get with" the Virginia governor to attempt to alter the power thrust from the combined governors. Arpert figured the governor would anticipate this and get somewhere safe. As a student of Virginia history, Arpert reveled in the challenge to figure it out. The governor would need media contact and his entourage of aides, but he would need to be free of obstruction from Petrarch. What would the U.S. military stationed in Virginia do?

Just then the radio was interrupted by an announcement from General Petrarch:

"Fellow Americans, this is General Petrarch. As you know we are in a national crisis, and in this, as in any other emergency, public safety is of paramount concern. Already we have suppressed anarchy threatening our safety in and around the City of Baltimore. We now have that city, and the District of Columbia, under strict martial law. I feel certain the incidence of violence in those areas under military authority will subside, and our citizens will be safer. Additionally our intelligence efforts are seeking to interdict any attempts to terrorize or mislead the public. Our forces are reaching major cities across the Eastern U.S., and we will expand our efforts as time, security and resources allow.

"I want to thank the American people for observing the security protocol I have established, including the 9:00 p.m. curfew, and we appreciate any information you can call in to our command centers on any terroristic activities. Rest assured I will keep you informed as best I can. Thank you."

Arpert didn't even wait for the gasp to follow this announcement from the talk show host. He reached to punch off the car radio. Just before the signal quit, he heard the disgusted gasp anyhow.

Arpert had a hunch he knew where the governor was. He called his wife, left a voicemail that he'd be late getting home, and that he would call her back. Arpert checked his rear-view mirrors, put on the left turn signal, and pulled out into traffic. He headed for the beltway. The Diet Coke was good.

The sound was throbbing, deep, horror-filled. Almost exhaling, saturating the hallway with a paralyzing dread. Deeper, harder the throb struck the core of every being clinging to the rectory floor. Erik could not begin to identify this experience in military or behavioral terms--he had no human experience as an anchor. What pulled so deep and hard at one's heart and mind and struck with so much fear? Aching with worry, Erik lifted up and could only make out a huge, dark smudge moving about the rooms. The sound grabbed deeper into his body as the darkness moved over the clutch of bodies on the rectory floor. What projection was this? Was this paranoid imagination run rampant? Was their shared fear of death enough to summon this mass?

Erik, seldom afraid, even in combat, was terror-stricken. He was losing his bearings--he even wondered if he'd be better off dead--all of them!

The grip of this entity--psychological or physical--was beyond description. Suddenly the sobbing group of people was convulsed with muscle spasms from legs to neck in violent waves. And laughter--hideous, ridiculing laughter--of every octave and voice, echoed through the building. Erik forced his eyes over toward his wife and daughter--theirs searched for his for help--PLEASE-- help!

Olive's eyes went suddenly from fear to serenity--her body quit convulsing, and she relaxed. Then she closed her eyes, and with a knowing, confident smile she embraced her boy--who then also relaxed. Then she enveloped Erik's wife and daughter and all the others one by one until they each were rescued from the terror…and found peace. Erik, still gripped by THE THING writhed in agony until HE GOT IT.

"Jesus, RELEASE me from this evil!" And Erik slumped in total release and peace to the floor.

Utterly amazed-- the dozen worshippers lifted their eyes to see Christ standing before them, smiling with eyes that told everything! We are saved! Christ nodded in the affirmative and walked the black mist--the evil entity right out of the walls of the home. Silence. Peace. Total JOY!

Father Sperry was used to telling everyone he met the way it was SUPPOSED to be. He carried the kind of air of cleric authority that superseded the surface portrayal of a priest. Yes, he wore the black outfit and white collar uniform that trumpeted his presence. Yes, he gave the dull stare, pursed lips and gaze beyond the person talking with him as if communicating with far more important issues beyond. Diminished as that made one feel, Sperry still communicated a depth--a depth of connectedness to the Depths and Heights of the SPIRIT. Father Sperry was at once predictable and dominant, but also in touch with God's universe. An annoying finality.

This was a problem for the detention facility. This was NOT just any rabble-rouser. Sperry was well-known in town for his political as well as social views. He publicly praised the freedoms promised through fidelity to Jesus Christ with the freedoms pushed for by TEA PARTIERS. This fractious platform set Sperry apart from the other ministerium --most were fat, happy tenders of their flocks, content to spread salve rather than to open wounds. Sperry did it all. He left no one unchallenged.

Father Sperry's reputation as a scrapper did not prepare him for the devastation he felt. Having been KIDNAPPED after being ATTACKED without CAUSE paled next to the morbid fear he harbored after hearing the shots fired about his church. WHAT IN GOD'S NAME HAD HAPPENED? WHO SHOT AT WHAT OR WHOM? WHY WERE THERE NO SCREAMS? WHAT ABOUT OLIVE, HIS BOY? AND THE PRAYING AND PRAISING FOLK AT THE GATHERING? Sperry's stomach churned acid, and he thought he might throw up. Sperry's head was splitting--not even the blows he'd received would have caused this much pain.

"GUARD--OFFICER!" gurgled Father Sperry. He saw the shadow move down the hall. Maybe some help.

"Yes, Father Sperry?" asked the jailer.

"Something--anything--can you get me something for the acid in my stomach and the pain in my head?" he pleaded.

"Sure, Padre--we'll get you a "Bromo" or something."

Sperry's mind flashed to the image of the BROMO-SELTZER TOWER, a knock-off Italian campanile, in Baltimore. The trite association sickened him more.

Father Sperry needed relief--but beyond that he needed answers--fast! Somehow he believed that the faster he did something--ANYTHING--the better the chances he could get back with his family and flock. The seltzer came---Sperry downed it trying not to regurgitate. A few staccato burps, and he felt he could focus, and talk.

"Officer--could you help me again, please? [the guard walked up] Thank you for the medicine; it helped a lot. But could you please take me to speak with your shift commander? Or someone who can speak to me about what is happening?"

"You don't have much chance of that at this hour, sir. The place is filling up fast--the ARMY is seeing to THAT--and the brass is all flustered. I'd say you'd do better writing down your concerns and letting me turn 'em over to the case manager in the morning."

Sperry knew this was going to be an exercise in futility, but he nodded agreement just to be able to express his thoughts at all. He hoped for enough paper to start journaling as well. He cannily thought his recollections might help bring him justice down the line.

The jailer brought Father Sperry a short pencil (one that couldn't stab a guard too deeply) and a ruled tablet. Lots of paper! Sperry began to write. He'd sharpen that pencil on the concrete as needed. He wouldn't waste a grain of graphite asking to get the thing sharpened again. Now to focus.

Arpert got about as far as the exit to Shirley Highway off of Interstate-495 when he saw the traffic backing up. Off down the ramp he saw military vehicles--uniformed people reaching into cars--and passengers getting out. Arpert knew he didn't want to sit in that line. Further he knew--even if queried about his intended travel --he didn't want to have to fabricate a lie about where he was headed. He instinctively knew he didn't have much time if he was going to reach Virginia's governor. The military machine would slow him effortlessly.

Arpert hit his left blinker and melted back into traffic. He'd have to get off on some local street, wend his way from town to town on roads full of stoplights until he reached the spot. This would take time and finesse, looking like he was just moving from here to there--without signaling his intent to travel south. He knew that drivers communicate their intent long before committing to a lane or direction, that an observer can see it in one's style of driving.

Arpert wanted to give away nothing. To do this he intentionally let his mind go blank. He concentrated on things like groceries, filling the gas tank, walking the dog. Arpert's Maryland plates might give some authority cause to wave him over, and he would try to bluff mentally before he had to do any explaining.

At the first innocuous exit, Arpert pulled off and sat at a stop light. Military vehicles rushed past. No standing-out here, he thought to himself. So he inched and plodded and wound his way south parallel to the main I-95 artery.

Josi awoke again to find a well-dressed administrative-looking lady smiling over her.

"Josi, the governor would like you to join him if that's O.K."

"Who are YOU?" asked Josi suspiciously.

The woman pulled out a security badge from inside her jacket. It was still attached to a cord around her neck.

"One of the governor's assistants", she replied with a smile.

"Well, where is everyone, and why did I stay HERE, and why were those ARMY-GUYS looking for the governor? They say he's in danger!"

"Only in danger if he's forced to relinquish command, Josi. This is a struggle for power going on--a struggle between a shattered federal government and the resurgent States. The States have no intention of allowing an illegal federal authority to run things. Again.

"This has happened differently in our history before: for example under Lincoln and his War Department. Although the history books spoke glowingly of it, we suffered for it. The federal government became a state all unto itself. It was self-nourishing, self-sustaining, self-justifying regardless of consequences. It got away from the American people and our duly-elected representatives. This "solar flare" with General Petrarch is just a symptom of the sick-thinking that led our country away from the CONSENT OF THE GOVERNED to form a central power that decided everything for the American people. When was the last time you agreed with your taxes?"

"I can't remember ever feeling anything but held down and robbed by government taxes", claimed Josi.

"And did you speak out?" asked the assistant.

"Never--the IRS sent warnings and threats to take what we own so I never dared--"

SHE GOT IT.

"Josi, the governors would like to try a fresh start in America--a fresh start with a dear old document--the Constitution. They have moved to a safe location and will be in session soon. The Virginia governor asked for you by name. He likes your style--he likes your work--he'd like you to be a part of history."

"Please take me to him," assented Josi.

Erik decided it was safe at last to stand up, dust himself off and look out the windows of the rectory. It was daylight, and the dust seemed to have settled outside. At least there were no vehicles left in sight. Erik asked the dozen folks present to please stay close to the house--get some tea and food--but keep it down until he returned. He just wanted to reconnoiter before they discussed what to do next. The stunning vision of Christ escorting the devil off the premises still had everyone in a hushed state of ecstasy.

Erik eased open the front door and peered over the porch railing toward the front door of the church. Not even a squad car. What about all those people? Erik walked cautiously down the driveway to the front of the church, checking every inch of property along the way. The turf was torn up in every direction --evidence of tracked vehicles and deep-treaded Hummers. Other than that--the place was empty. Erik walked around the front and through the blown-out walls into the sanctuary. Shattered glass, splintered wood, crumbling masonry --prayer books and hymnals blown to shreds--there were people here last night--standing room only! Yet not one drop of blood anywhere! No bodies--no personal effects. Erik marveled at the selective clean-up job. What had God wrought in the face of this great evil?

Arpert pulled into the 7-11 off the by-way. It was Diet Coke time....he grabbed a cold half-liter bottle and a pack of nuts. Arpert was on the trail--he knew it. In the car he twisted off the bottle cap and took a huge gulp. This brought an involuntary hiccup--then another. Arpert opened the foil pack of nuts with his teeth and downed half the pack. He needed the energy. He had a lot of finessing ahead.

Arpert pulled out onto the road and headed south. Sideways he could see I-95 traffic backed up STILL--and he saw occasional troop carriers move down the shoulders. He marveled that the main highway was strangled by federal troops, but a perfectly good by-way was wide-open to traffic, unfettered and free. Such was the master thinking of the federal authority. Arpert kept his eyes on the signs looming before him. Soon I-95 moved away from his view. He concentrated on the prize: the white-lettered brown historical sign. The sign indicating a shrine--a shrine to southern knighthood.

Josi was driven up the small roads north of Richmond in a Toyota Yaris. She'd never ridden in one before, and she found it remarkably comfortable for its size. The car was decidedly low-profile--even the color, red, was so mainstream that the car never stood out. The license plates were vanity plates, however, and DA BABE flashed down the roads and around corners with scarcely a second look. Josi asked where they were headed. The administrative assistant said,"The Jackson Shrine".

"What's that?" asked Josi searching her memory for an Andrew Jackson shrine in Virginia.

"Where Stonewall Jackson died, my dear! It's a favorite stop for Civil War buffs and holy ground, let me tell you, for this governor!"

"Does General Petrarch suspect?" asked Josi nervously.

"Not yet, it would seem, and let's hope not today at least---the governor would really have to shift gears if he showed up."

Soon Josi was being driven into a parking area with a smattering of other very common vehicles..mostly Japanese. Another decoy. When they parked Josi got out of the Yaris and closed the door.

"Gosh, I'm famished--I should have asked you to pull into that 7-11 back there."

"No problem, Josi, there's plenty to eat inside", said the assistant. And with that Josi was escorted into the humble home where General Thomas Jackson died during the Chancellorsville campaign in 1863. Several tables were set up with great-looking cold cuts and all the fixins'. The Virginia Governor approached Josi saying, "THANKS for coming--please help yourself to food and drink----it's been a long couple of days, and it's about to get longer." He warmly smiled as he took her by the hand and led her to a stack of paper plates and napkins.

Josi didn't miss a beat--she was too tired and excited to deny herself sustenance. With an accomplished DAGWOOD sandwich in her lap she chewed while being briefed:

SEVERAL HEADS OF STATE HAVE ARRIVED STATESIDE AND WILL CONVERGE HERE WITHIN HOURS. PETRARCH IS AWARE OF THEIR ARRIVAL, BUT THEY ARE USING ALL MEANS AT THEIR DISPOSAL TO COME HERE UNDETECTED. THE COMBINED GOVERNORS WILL ARRIVE SIMULTANEOUSLY, AND AN EMERGENCY MEETING IS TO BE HELD TO PLAN THE NEXT MOVE. OUR GOVERNOR WANTED YOU TO BE HERE TO DOCUMENT THE EVENT. NO OTHER MEDIA WILL BE ALERTED.

"What if Petrarch crashes the party? Won't his people get suspicious of this Toyota convention?" quipped Josi.

"Since we are just about on the anniversary of the Chancellorsville battle we've decided to play the part."

"What do you mean?"

"Everyone, including you, Josi, will be dressed, accoutered, and armed like Civil War re-enactors!"

"Brilliant!" shrieked Josi.

Arpert was aware that he'd brought along his Confederate infantryman gear. Right down to his tattered socks, duct-taped brogans and finger-less gloves. He always kept his reproduction Enfield rifle in his trunk. He didn't give a DAMN about school rules on the matter. He was a HISTORY teacher, and by God, he'd LIVED the part as a re-enactor.

Arpert pulled over by the side of the road, and with his door opened facing the woods, started switching centuries. Before he knew it several groups of cars started heading his way, and he could see Confederate gray and Union blue kepi's bobbing in the seats as the cars rushed by.

"Looks like those fellahs got new wheels," thought Arpert--most re-enactors drove well-worn cars and pick-up trucks festooned with stickers like HISTORY, NOT HATE under the Confederate battle flag or MY ANCESTOR SHOT YOUR ANCESTOR with flags from both north and south on the same sticker. The company of re-enactors was always generous to Arpert, and he felt right at home in almost any camp.

Slouching his kepi on his head and pulling his suspenders up over his shoulders, Arpert got back behind the wheel and sped south, tightly following the group of cars of re-enactors.

"Strange", thought Arpert, "how Yankees got in the same cars as Rebs in so many of those vehicles". The company of opposing soldiers was never an issue as both sides got along famously, though units from one side or another would usually not travel together.

"Maybe it's a movie-shoot!" marveled Arpert. "Maybe they need extras!" All of a sudden Arpert's drive to find Virginia's governor was energized by the added bonus of finding a movie set. Even with the world turned upside-down--Civil War documentaries must go on, he fantasized!

With renewed vigor Arpert closed the distance on the soldiers speeding along ahead. He knew they were approaching Chancellorsville, and he prepared to turn with them. As if on cue, each of the cars ahead turned left up the road headed to the battlefield. Arpert was packed right in there with them!

Josi was trying on several 19th century-style reproduction camp dresses and stepped out for the others to see.

"Beautiful!" exclaimed the Virginia Governor, now dressed as an artillery private from the Army of Northern Virginia.

"You look like you BELONG in this century, Josi!"

Josi beamed. She stepped outside to find dozens of Civil War-style tents going up, including one huge "meeting tent". The camp was festooned with flags from the period-- both north and south, Josi surmised. It looked for all the world like a re-enactment Josi had seen on T.V.

Josi studied the faces of the men and women dressed in 19th-century garb. Some were from other parts of the globe and yes, there were the other governors she'd recognized from the night before. As she studied the crowd it became clear that dignitaries were dressed as privates and servants and their assistants were dressed as officers and ladies! The ruse was complete. Soon Josi heard a fiddle, guitar and banjo emanating from the meeting tent, and the crowd began to gather.

The erstwhile business-like administrative assistant came up dressed in great finery with a parasol.

"Josi, here are your tools of the trade--let's get to work!"

Josi followed eagerly.

Arpert followed the re-enactors' cars right up the road. Fortunately they were headed in the direction he'd hoped--the Jackson Shrine! By golly, they all wheeled into the same parking area, and there were tents, flags-- BIG DOINGS! Arpert didn't know exactly what was up, but he followed right along and parked. Soldiers and ladies all exited their cars and were pointed toward the big tent. Some wore leathers that were used to hold weapons and brass buckles in the War, most didn't. None carried weapons from their cars yet, so Arpert left his rifle in the trunk of his car. That aside, Arpert was fully decked-out, as raunchy as any Confederate private in history. Arpert hated being a FARB (an inauthentic re-enactor), and aside from his duct-tapes shoes, he was every inch authentic. Lice would have placed him in the moment.

Arpert noticed pretty quickly that all these soldiers were clad in spanking-new uniforms. No one seemed to have been in the field yet where the sun would have left its mark over time. Now he was having doubts--was this a "fresh-fish" orientation? He'd have a look-see.

As Arpert moved into the meeting tent the crowd eyed the stage with eagerness. Some looked about chatting appreciatively at each-others' get-ups, but some took in Arpert's dishevelment with a jaundiced eye. What was this? This couldn't be what he was looking for. Arpert turned to leave when suddenly a familiar voice spoke into the microphone--tapping and saying: "Testing, testing". Arpert whipped around---PAY DIRT!

Josi was positioned on the stage behind Virginia's mike-tapping governor. The crowd roared approval, and the governor announced his Civil War name and rank. More cheers. The governor chuckled about the assembly looking perfect for a Civil War-era ball and suggested they have one just as soon as their business was concluded.

JUST THEN-- Humvees stormed the parking lot, and soldiers with automatic weapons circled the gathering. Josi gasped.

"Relax, folks," chuckled the governor, "and please welcome the VIRGINIA DEFENSE FORCE, they're with me!" More cheers erupted, and the governor clapped his approval of these fine Virginia militia here to protect the Commonwealth's interests.

"Now then. There will be food and music later--and yes, dancing, I am told! You all look so wonderful! You know--a very great man died on this property almost 150 years ago. Thomas "Stonewall" Jackson, Robert E. Lee's 2nd Corps commander, was wounded, fell ill with pneumonia, and died right over there in that house".

Josi blushed as she had changed in there. She could not explain the feeling.

"General Jackson died on a Sunday, something he said he wanted to do. He died a contented man, they say, a man knowing he'd given it his ALL to defend the freedoms accorded his people by the Constitution of the United States. Jackson was oft quoted when asked how to treat the invaders of his state's soil: 'Give them the BLACK FLAG', meaning give them no quarter--kill them all.

"You see General Jackson was a devout Christian who held his hand up to praise God even in the middle of the most desperate of battles when lead iron flew all about him. When asked why he took such chances, he responded that he was as safe in battle as he was in bed on a Sunday morning. His faith was not delusional. Jackson was wounded by accident by his own men after the battle's work had been done that day. Jackson's time was up. He strongly believed that he had served God's purpose and well.

"No, General Jackson did not order the BLACK FLAG to be cruel; he recognized that the numerically-superior invading tyrant needed to be taught a lesson---a lesson in Constitutional government--a lesson that Thomas Jefferson spoke so eloquently when he suggested that a truly free people should arm themselves AGAINST the government, just should it go the way of tyranny.

"And yes, unpopular is this thought, given our history school texts, but Abraham Lincoln was a tyrant in this way: he chose to subvert the sovereign will of the people. He subverted law and popular sovereignty in both the North and the South for a cause he and his backers believed in: central power.

"Today, friends, we witness the ruin of that work in our bombed-out nation's capital. We face the fierce remanent of Sherman's army in General Petrarch --a man who believes in his cause, but it's a cause that trumps the will of the people in his own mind. We see this clearly in his late actions around Baltimore.

"If you look around this tent", continued Virginia's governor, you will see many familiar faces and some new faces as well. Forty-nine governors are present [cheering]--and while many foreign diplomats were sadly killed in the blast on the Mall in Washington, we have managed to gather new diplomats from some 55 different nations here today! [cheers and applause] Thank you, Ladies and Gentlemen! Thank you for coming, and thank you, for you inspire us in our cause! [whooping and cheering]

"We will not give up! American will rise from these ashes, helped by our neighbors of good will, and we will overcome the vestiges of tyranny here at home. We will assemble, vote, assemble again and rebuild our precious nation! [cheers] We governors, senators, and representatives surviving from all 50 states are committed to this work!

"So before we party tonight on this sacred ground--let us get to our delegations and conduct some business. I am grateful that you all were willing to dress your part tonight--apparently General Petrarch never guessed it was you!"

Josi's hands were trembling by now---she was awed by this man's gravity. She was also deeply grateful to be there.

Arpert took in the Virginia governor's opening speech with relish. Man, he thought, he really NAILED it when he found this place. He felt he was right where he wanted to be today in HISTORY. He planned to make the most of it! But first---a little perimeter patrol--he smelled a rat.

Father Sperry wrote until his pencil died; he pestered for an additional pencil, and finally a third. After that, he divined he'd worn out his welcome with the guard. In spite of his annoyance, the guard came down to ask Sperry if he was OK.

"My son," started Sperry, "it is not you who have sinned. It is the hand that feeds you. I do not hold you in contempt. We are all afflicted by the tyranny at hand."

"Tell me about it!" sheepishly responded the guard.

"You agree?" hoped Sperry.

Looking right to left and lowering his voice even further the guard kept his professional distance but intimated, "Sir, we are on live camera but are not bugged. Therefore I will try to look like I am just giving you orders and all. But I can assure you, Father, I and many others are against this takeover and all these jailings. We just don't know what to do!"

"Have you all talked about civil disobedience?" asked Sperry.

"What would that be?" asked the guard desperately. "The governor's gone---the mayor of Baltimore is gone---the chief of police is a worthless puppet--heck Washington and Annapolis both are ghost towns to hear of it--who can take charge besides this General Petrarch?" He looked despondent. "We don't know anything else to do, sir!"

Father Sperry, lit with anticipation, asked, "Did you boys ever study the Constitution of the Unites States in school?"

"Sir, I think it had something to do with the Declaration of Independence or something with Benjamin Franklin. Anyhow, it's the law of the land, I know THAT," offered the guard.

"Yes, and it stands as a protection for the people of our great country AGAINST any tyrant who should try to take over," said Sperry.

"How do you mean?"

"It provides citizens, yourself included, the guarantee that you can--NO, that you SHOULD--take up arms against any tyrant who tries to shut down our democracy".

"And by that you mean----?"

"Yes, what happened to those people peacefully assembled at my church was just such an act of tyranny!", asserted Sperry.

" But the news has it you were leading an act of rebellion to overthrow martial law", offered the guard.

"Look, no such thing happened--we were gathered praying, praising God, healing--God was bringing HIS PEOPLE together spontaneously in this desperate time!"

"But the reports have it you violated curfew."

"Son, we had no knowledge of any curfew--we'd been there most of the day, and it was surely dark outside when the troops surrounded the church and demanded we--"

"CORPORAL!" blurted the loudspeaker in the hallway. "Report to the lieutenant's office!"

"Sorry, Father, gotta go---eyes watching, you know."

Father Sperry watched the young guard get buzzed out of the holding-cell area. Sperry had hope--hope he'd reached the kid--HOPE he'd pull up the Bill of Rights and read them!

Arpert pulled away from the gathering of re-enactors and went for his rifle in the back of the car. He had blank powder cartridges and all his gear in his cartridge box and haversack. As he slipped into the woodbine past the parking lot he looked every bit ephemera--his aging gait and gray beard only adding to the picture of a Confederate ghost in the twilight. He walked softly... softly but deliberately through the deeper shades of woods --further out the perimeter of the event.

Suddenly Arpert spotted them--modern military men stood out in desert cammo in these darkening woods. Arpert froze--then did the deliberate, well-rehearsed walk of a 19th-century guard on picket duty. As if unaware of their presence--as if fixed on an ancient duty called upon to walk from age to age--Arpert simply moved in stealth--but plain view--right past these men.

"Holy SHIT! Will you look at that? That one ain't wearing no new uniform! He doesn't even see us! My God! It's the REAL thing!" whisper-shrieked the squad leader.

"A real REB GHOST! This place is just as haunted as they said! Let's get the hell out of here!" pleaded a private.

Arpert kept walking through--just far enough away --to tempt fantasy.

"Pull back, men!" ordered the squad leader. With this the desert-cammo-clad troops from Petrarch's command withdrew without the intel they were hoping to confirm. "Looks like we were given a false lead--mount up--let's go!"

Arpert moved into some dense brush to become as invisible as he could. He cut his eyes only to confirm the squad's withdrawal. When he was certain they were gone a huge smile spread across his face---"I haven't felt this good in years!"

Arpert had cemented his place in history.

Erik went back to the rectory to find the folks there eating and getting caught up.

"Folks--looks like all's clear. The church has been shelled--I have NO evidence of casualties--everybody is gone!"

" You mean there's no blood or clothing or anything?" asked Erik's wife incredulously.

"That's what I'm here to tell you--- it's a miracle. The church was shattered in several places--but NO evidence of loss of life--I doubt anyone could have cleaned up THAT effectively overnight", said Erik. "I think God has touched us twice in one night!"

"Well, what's next?" asked one of the ladies sipping tea.

"Well, I for one want to find Father Sperry--he should be able to shed some light on all this," said Erik.

With that, Olive smiled broadly and asked, "And he's no doubt giving SOMEBODY in charge a piece of his mind!"

"Let's see, if they took him, where would they be holding him?" thought Erik out loud.

"I have a hunch maybe it's where they had THIS ONE the other day!" Olive grinned and pointed at her boy.

The lad lowered his head and said with a sheepish grin, "yeah, I'll bet Dad's giving them HECK!"

"Olive, shall we take the Corolla?" asked Erik.

"Sure, I'll drive--I know the way".

"My thoughts exactly," said Erik. Erik asked his wife to stay with the others while he and Olive went hunting for Father Sperry. Olive's boy came along--he wasn't going to miss this for anything.

Arpert was heading through the woods back to the main event when he heard voices off to the left. Twilight was fading fast into darkness, and Arpert was getting slightly disoriented. He headed for the sound of voices.

Then he saw it---a campfire crackling with a tripod supporting a large coffee pot. The voices around the fire were course and distinctly southern--Arpert hadn't heard that exact accent before--he was sure.

Arpert announced himself and stepped forward. The gathering of soldiers looked up at him, and waved him forward after checking him over once or twice. Broad, toothy smiles and expectant faces greeted Arpert as he checked his footing and began to move in their direction. When he lifted his face to greet the men, they began to fade. Arpert blinked and eagerly moved in their direction only to step into a clearing with a cold, ancient firepit. Arpert's head was spinning. He pinched his leg--he was awake there alright!

This was a moment he'd never forget--and likely never tell of. He smiled and was deeply grateful for the honor.

Father Sperry heard the electronic gate buzz, and he looked up. In stepped the young jailer, only he had Olive and his son in tow!

"Well hello, and praise the Lord!" shouted Sperry. Grinning from ear to ear Sperry was just so grateful to see his family ALIVE! Erik walked in right behind them.

"Uh, Father Sperry-- we've come to 'visit', and, uh, see what needs to be done to get you out of here", said Erik. Olive just smiled and took Sperry's hands through the bars. Obviously visiting rules had been relaxed! Sperry's boy reached through the bars also, and with Sperry starting them off, the three of them launched into singing:

AMAZING GRACE--HOW SWEET THE SOUND--THAT SAVED A WRETCH LIKE ME---I ONCE WAS LOST---BUT NOW AM FOUND---WAS BLIND, BUT NOW I SEE.

Now the jailer and Erik joined clumsily in:

'TWAS GRACE THAT TAUGHT MY HEART TO FEAR---AND GRACE MY FEARS RELIEVED--- HOW PRECIOUS DID THAT GRACE APPEAR--THE HOUR I FIRST BELIEVED.

THROUGH MANY DANGERS, TOILS AND SNARES--I HAVE ALREADY COME--

…and suddenly the earth shook--and shook the jail violently--but the singers kept their poise, held gently in balance on their feet-- when

CRASH-- the doors all popped open and stood open wide.

The wide-eyed corporal exclaimed, "It was God's hand--let's GO!"

And with that Father Sperry, Olive, their boy, Erik, the corporal and the entire staff of the jail emptied with the erstwhile incarcerated into the parking lot.

The shift commander walked up to a stunned Father Sperry and said, "Like with Silas and Paul, the gates were opened…Father, we know our duties to the people of this state under our Constitution. Please take these keys to the bus, get your people back at your church and neighborhood, and take them where they need to go. The bus can be returned when it is convenient for you---we've inconvenienced you plenty!"

"Bless you, sir!" shouted Father Sperry.

Sperry motioned for any who would come to jump into the bus. Olive, their boy, and Erik were joined by several others who'd been swept up by Petrarch's troops, and Sperry vowed to get them home.

Father Sperry started to get behind the wheel of the County Corrections' bus then realized he wasn't skilled at driving such a vehicle. The corporal motioned to be allowed up and said, "I got permission to drive you wherever you need and got a gas card to boot!"

With that the officer got behind the wheel of the bus and cranked her up. Father Sperry stood up front and held his hands over the passengers, and raising his eyes to heaven said, "Father, for your limitless blessings we give thanks!" The bus backed up, and Sperry plopped down next to the driver as he roared up the road.

Along the highway to Sperry's church General Petrarch's army had check points. At each stop the guard simply offered a wave, and the troops passed him swiftly along. This was going to be smooth. Along the way Erik briefed Father Sperry about what he'd witnessed at the rectory and the church since he'd been taken away. Sperry's jaw dropped--"You mean Christ cast out the devil?!"

"Walked him RIGHT out of your home!"

"And there was no blood in the church pews or aisles or grounds this morning?"

"Absolutely NO sign of people dead, alive, bleeding or blown apart", said Erik, "and I know what I'm looking for!"

"Indeed you do, Erik!--a miracle---God took those souls and held them safe in HIS bosom! I am sure of it! A miracle! The devil may rant and rave and try to take over, but he has NO power over GOD'S FAITHFUL! Oh, praise the Lord!" Sperry was never so ALIVE! Tears streaming down his face, Sperry directed the corporal toward his rectory.

Josi was enjoying the ball after the dignitaries had met in session. From everything she'd recorded that day it was clear that a new Congress was to be formed, and the combined governors assured one another that local guard forces would make safe the elections. Dates were worked on, and practical sharing of resources were worked through.

The Governor of Virginia was the center of gravity here, it was certain. But he made no noises about running ANYTHING other than his own state and his temporary charges including Maryland and D.C. He made it clear to all gathered that he would not run head-long into General Petrarch nor call him out in any way. Humbly, prayerfully, he said he would summon the armed forces at his disposal as he needed them only. And to date, no base commander had refused him. Yes, General Petrarch's men were out there, but they were increasingly irrelevant. National Guard, Virginia Defense Force, Army, Navy, Air Force and Marines all were coming over to the governor. Soon this hiding would be unnecessary.

Josi felt a deep sense of pride at this place, time and event. She never dreamed she'd be included like this in anything so important in her life. Then again, Christ was the Great Architect, and she's served HIM for years before! That His work would come alive so completely in her life should not have, and really wasn't, a great surprise. She felt complete gratitude.

Father Sperry's Corrections bus wheeled into the parking lot between the church and the rectory. Sperry, Erik, and Olive went inside and gathered Erik's wife, daughter and the others worshippers together. While the bus sat idling outside, and the prison corporal used the bathroom, Father Sperry spoke to the small gathering:

"Friends of Christ! You have witnessed a great miracle right here! I will tell you of another if you will join me on a bit of a trek down to Virginia . I can assure you Christ is guiding us, and riding WITH us!

"I believe God took all the worshippers the troops had surrounded and shelled here last night. I believe God swept them up in His arms--hairpins, wallets and all to send us a sign: a sign that Christ will vanquish the evil one, and that our cause is HIS cause! Erik here has a real good notion that General Petrarch will start a crack down that we would do well to miss here in Maryland. His suggestion, and one that I endorse, is to head well into Virginia where the Virginia governor is bringing democracy back to the people. Our escort--the County Corrections Department and the good corporal here --just returned from the head-- is willing to take us where we feel we will be safe. I know a church down I-95 north of Richmond that would befriend us all in a heartbeat. I can't wait to tell you what happened to us down at the jail! Are you with us?" [the group nodded general assent]

Folks all loaded on the bus, and the corporal speeding south on I-695 toward I-95, Father Sperry regaled the small group with his tale of AMAZING GRACE.

General Petrarch was monitoring troop deployments and "civil unrest" up and down the cities of the Northeast. He'd clearly lost his grip on Virginia and points south, and he was exploring options on regaining control of the main bases, when an aide interrupted with news of a suspect "Civil War Re-Enactment" in Chancellorsville, Virginia. Apparently a squad was poking around looking for the Virginia governor on a tip, and came across a lot of soldiers encamped and celebrating something. The squad "couldn't" get close enough to confirm or deny the governor's presence because the Virginia Defense Force was thick. They were given orders not to assault or probe enough to be seen.

"Damn fools!" cried Petrarch. "The battle of Chancellorsville is being re-enacted this weekend! It is this time EVERY year! Why the HELL are you wasting my time with this--and worse yet, risking our operation chasing ghosts?! Get out of here and find me something operational!"

No one had even mentioned the ghost.

General Petrarch wasn't a praying man, but he was involved in something very personal, focused and other-worldly. Petrarch followed mythology, and he'd been convinced after years in the Middle East that local rituals and supplications to the pre-Islamic deities had power. He'd seen men and women die suddenly after ritual spells, and he'd seen entire villages swayed by the shamanic trances conjured to influence local events.

General Petrarch wanted to harness those forces. He'd enlisted the help of an old soothsayer-shaman who, for a price and a lot of protection guarantees, got Petrarch into the practice of ritual "conjuring". The general became convinced over time that his new "contacts" with the beyond were winning him influence and strength with the local tribes. He believed his work was empowered and that he gained success through the spirits.

Now General Petrarch was conjuring stateside. He felt the power of certitude--he knew that taking control of this powerful nation was his calling--HIS FINEST HOUR! HE was the only man alive who could bring order to this CHAOS, and it was HIS moment--much like George Washington's--that would deliver him the White House. Only his new nation would know the benefit of decisive, no-nonsense leadership. Congress could wait. The Supreme Court could wait. Peace through strength---HIS strength was the prime directive of the day. The general's repeated contacts with the beyond led him to this moment. He would not be distracted.

Petrarch HAD to bring this rebellion in Virginia under control. But how to arrest Virginia's popular governor--all the governors--and how to find them? This Virginia Defense Force--this beer-swilling gadfly substitute for the National Guard--what were they doing? They were--they don't show up in force at Civil War Re-enactments---they had to be---"CHRIST!" Petrarch shouted, slamming his fist--they had to be hiding SOMETHING!

Darkness drew around General Petrarch as he encountered his cultivated "deities". To a casual observer he'd appear demented, obsessed, fanatical. In his safely secretive seance he felt he was in contact with the powers of the beyond--the essence of human spiritual strength and the source of all worldly power. Petrarch had a VISION that the Virginia governor was holding a subversive gathering of rebellious state leaders under the guise of a re-enactment--now taking place---under his nose--in Chancellorsville! Like the Civil War Union General Hooker, Petrarch felt confident he could CRUSH this rebel force and win national laurels in a swift victory! He summoned his aide and gathered his generals in conference. The strike was on!

Arpert went into the large gathering in the meeting tent and watched the gay proceedings. In another day and time, he would have been drinking heavily along with taking pharmaceuticals. Arpert had learned the hard way, through family tough love, that poisoning himself wasn't the gateway to spiritual bliss. With Sobriety Arpert found Christ near and dear. His every day was a tribute to Christ's teachings--he'd seen to it that his devotions were thorough and regular. Tonight Arpert prayed for deliverance for all the gathered guests --and mostly that all would do Christ's work.

Josi found time for relaxation once the secretarial pressures relented for the day. She collapsed into a comfortable chair at the Civil War military ball and watched the gathering with a deep sense of history. Bowing her head in gratitude, she thanked God for all his blessings--this opportunity to serve in the cause of FREEDOM--this chance to contribute--to be at the peak of her performance in the greatest cause she could imagine. Josi shut her eyes glowing with pride.

The Corrections corporal had cleared the checkpoints on I-95 in Maryland and was making time down Shirley Highway. The dozen-plus worshippers were singing A MIGHTY FORTRESS IS OUR GOD when the corporal spotted something in his rearview mirror that he found startling:

Tanks, armored-personnel carriers, and Humvees racing down the same highway in THEIR direction and at amazing speed! Civilian vehicles were pulling over to get out of the way. The corporal called Erik up to the front of the bus and pointed this out. Erik showed Father Sperry. The three of them decided to get off I-95 and take a parallel route and let this force pass---

---

General Petrarch was in the vanguard of his mobilized troops heading south on I-95. His Humvee was making excellent time as traffic south all got out of the way. The APC's, tanks and fuel trucks all kept pace--it was an awesome and fearsome sight. Petrarch was coordinating with his remaining generals. He wanted this to go precisely--he demanded that the Chancellorsville event get surrounded--Virginia Defense Force and all---and no one allowed in or out. As he raced south, Petrarch became focused--a reddening face and trance-like fierceness kept his aides from interrupting. General Petrarch was going to crush this rebellion! The glow off the dashboard instrument panel reflected on the general's face only served to terrify his driver. This was surely unnatural.

The Virginia governor was clapping and stomping his feet in the main tent, thrilling to the 19th-century music. He was about to ask his administrative assistant for the next dance when three members of the Virginia Defense Force breached the opening to the tent and looked about for the governor. When they saw him--they moved quickly in his direction. The governor spotted them and motioned them over to the side so as to minimize the drama.

"Sir, we have intercepted transmissions from General Petrarch's forces indicating that he is bringing a large force of armored vehicles to Chancellorsville to find you and the 'rogue' governors".

"What is their estimated time of arrival, Colonel?" asked the governor stoicly.

"Sir, they sound like they are practically upon us--we haven't seen any air traffic in support---I think they are trying to take us by surprise. Sir, do you want us to set up a counter-strike?" asked the colonel as if volunteering to commit suicide.

"That would be suicide, colonel. NO way, thanks, but no way! We will put our trust in the Lord--have your men and women stand down--no, better yet--have them join us in here---"

"But sir, we risk--" blurted the VDF officer.

"TRUST--trust and pray with us!" assured the governor.

The governor made his way slowly up to the scruffy band and motioned for them to wind down. He signaled appreciation and took the stage and the microphone.

"Thank you, 42nd Tennessee String Band! Let's give 'em a big cheer, folks! [cheers and applause] Folks, this has been a RED LETTER DAY--we've feasted, danced--we've brought America closer to the democracy our forefathers fought for than this continent has witnessed in fifteen decades! [cheers]

"Now it is time to pray. We have done our work here--and now we must give thanks and pray to God that He will deliver us--and our efforts--from the hands of the enemy--so that this great work will be done!"

And Arpert stood in the back, tears rolling down his cheeks, and bowed his head with the rest. Josi stood on the stage, put one arm around the smiling Virginia governor and raised her right hand to heaven. And the world was silent for this great moment.

Father Sperry watched out of the bus window as the corporal sped down the by-way running parallel to I-95. Erik was able to identify some of the vehicles running along next to them on the super highway.

"This is going to be some SHIN-DIG when they get where they are going," said Erik. "I wouldn't want to get in their way".

"A lot of worshippers already did, unawares, Erik. You smelled it coming, and you got these folks to safety. Think we can repeat that one?" asked Sperry.

"Now THAT would be a miracle!" said Erik.

"How are we going to know who they're targeting?" shouted the corporal.

"We'll stay with them, and if we can see them slow enough at an exit, we'll have a 50-50 chance of heading in the right direction ahead of them to find a gathering of people that MIGHT be targeted---it's a long-shot," said Erik.

"I will start a prayer to guide us--" inserted Father Sperry.

"Lord Jesus, only YOU know where this evil is headed--and only YOU know where to guide us--please, Dear Jesus, guide us to protect these people!"

"AMEN!", shouted the dozen in perfect unison.

Signs for Chancellorsville Battlefield loomed ahead--

Erik said, "O, my Gosh--I'll bet---there's a re-enactment this weekend-- I'll bet the Governor of Virginia is there!"

Sperry shot a glance to the right to confirm the suspicion--the armored vehicles were slowing--likely to make the Chancellorsville exit!

"Turn at the sign for the battlefield--they are headed to the gathering there!" shouted Sperry.

The corporal got to the intersection--looked both ways, and ran the light in a hard left turn. The passengers shrieked as they tossed to the right, but no one was hurt. The bus roared ahead.

They didn't have to get far--they saw the gathering tent off the road through the woods, and the bus tore into the parking lot. Erik and Sperry jumped out of the bus as soon as it slowed and sprinted up to the tent gathering.

Already the roar of heavy, tracked vehicles could be heard up the road and Sperry was NOT looking forward to a blood-bath!

The pair entered the big tent breathlessly only to see the mass of people dressed as Civil War re-enactors bowed in prayer.

As if infused with oxygen--sudden calm--great strength and a powerful understanding, Erik and Father Sperry sank to their knees and offered thanks to Jesus FOR WHAT HE WAS ABOUT TO DO!

General Petrarch was in a near-frenzy as he rounded the curve into the parking lot--the tent was well-illuminated. He shouted orders for the tanks to fan out to surround the gathering. The APC's deployed their cargo, and soldiers moved to shouted orders in all directions. The din and dust were horrifying. And the crowd in the tent did not move.

Gene was standing in His Presence--right next to Our Lord, Jesus Christ, so deeply in love and deeply grateful for his salvation!

"Gene--you were a polished speaker all your life-- a very influential man," said Jesus---"and it's your turn to make a great contribution to your people."

Gene was embarrassed knowing his life of platitudes and glad-handing and said, "Lord, I wasn't real though".

And Jesus said, "Well, this will be as real as it gets--all you need to do is stand before that man right there--the one with the black stars on his collar--and tell him you've come for him in MY NAME. Tell him he is to lay down his weapons and seek my face".

Gene said, "I would be HAPPY to help, Lord!"

"Then go", said Jesus.

General Petrarch stood triumphantly before his prey--the blackness within him seething with POWER. Breathlessly he raised one arm to signal the barrage when he suddenly he saw this man appear before him--

"I come in the NAME OF JESUS CHRIST! He says you shall lay down your weapons and seek His face! Brother, as one who has sinned--please join me and follow HIM!" implored Gene.

General Petrarch was frozen for a moment--tears flooded his eyes--and he dropped to his knees---"Yes, Lord Jesus, FREE ME!!" he emptied.

And the blackness left him and split the air like a sonic boom. Petrarch went limp, but raised an arm and shouted clearly to his men,

"In the Name of Jesus, CEASE FIRE!"

Laughing, crying, on all fours he began asking God for forgiveness. His aides rushed to his side, and he said, "These people are our brothers--let us join them now!"

STUNNED the commanders shut down their engines, and one by one each soldier stepped from their vehicles to the grass around the great tent. General Petrarch made it to his feet, and with help, got inside the tent and lifted the Virginia governor to his feet and embraced him.

"Jesus Saves!" he shouted to the sky. The crowd ROARED.

Arpert observed, "And once again, the lamb lay down with the lion!"

-------------------------------fin-------------------------------------

Copyright, James Eric Davison, November, 2010

Made in the USA
Columbia, SC
17 November 2023